Freemasonry Antichrist Quasi-Re
Occultism, Alzheimer's Disease,
English Law

Your Majesty, the fellow is who He says He is – John 14:6.

**CONTENTS:**

PROLOGUE: **11**

ONE: **16**

TWO: **21**

THREE: **28**

FOUR: **31**

FIVE: **39**

SIX: **45**

SEVEN: **48**

EIGHT: **52**

NINE: **60**

TEN: **74**

ELEVEN: **85**

TWELVE: **96**

THIRTEEN: **105**

FOURTEEN: **116**

FIFTEEN: **125**

SIXTEEN: **133**

SEVENTEEN: **144**

EIGHTEEN: **148**

NINETEEN: **156**

TWENTY: **162**

TWENTY-ONE: **173**

TWENTY-TWO: **181**

TWENTY-THREE: **187**

TWENTY-FOUR: **191**

TWENTY-FIVE: **196**

TWENTY-SIX: **207**

TWENTY-SEVEN: **215**

TWENTY-EIGHT: **223**

TWENTY-NINE: **227**

THIRTY: **233**

THIRTY-ONE: **237**

ABOUT THE AUTHOR: **246**

**PROLOGUE:** "There is not a truth existing which I fear or would wish unknown to the whole world." President Thomas Jefferson (1743–1826).

'Judiciary in England and Wales 'institutionally racist', says https://www.theguardian.com › law › oct › judiciary-[i...18 Oct 2022—Exclusive: more than half of legal professionals in survey said they saw a judge acting in a racially biased way.

Medium
https://medium.com/@ec770072/c-of-e-raises-serious-concerns-ab...
C of E raises serious concerns about Christian Freemasons.
WEB Nov 18, 2021 ·
If District Judge Paul Ayers of Bedford County Court, 3 St Paul's Square Bedford, MK40 9 DN, read the Judgement that he approved, he must be a fool. If he didn't, he must have lied as he ...
Your Majesty, Freemasons are Antichrist, vulgarly charitable, LIARS (John 8:44, John 10:10), and closeted White supremacist bastards, and they have unbounded and unaccountable illegal parallel power, which they use to guard MERCILESS RACIST EVIL—Habakkuk 1:4.

"Those who have the power to do wrong with impunity seldom wait long for the will." Dr Samuel Johnson

BEDFORD, ENGLAND: NHS/GDC, Freemason, Brother, Richard Hill fabricated reports and unrelentingly lied under oath—Habakkuk 1:4. A very, very, very, dishonest pure White man. A crooked closeted hereditary RACIST FREEMASON.

Freemasons: Vulgarly charitable, Antichrist, and Closeted White Supremacist evil pure White bastards (predominantly but not exclusively pure White) who do RACIAL HATRED 'legally' – Habakkuk. They are very, very, very, highly civilised, and super-enlightened, and they do everything legally, including RACIAL HATRED and FRAUD: Rules based procedures, precedent, and statute etcetera. Then, GREEDY BASTARDS won in crooked courts before crooked Judges, but in the WAR, when the physically ill-favoured homunculus Corporal flipped, the real Judge looked away, and greedy bastards lost everything and more – John 5:22, Matthew 25:31- 46. Facts are sacred, and they cannot be overstated.

BEDFORD, ENGLAND: Sue Gregory (OBE), alleged Rotarian (Freemasonry without voodoo and/or occultists' rituals) unrelentingly lied under implied oath and/or on record—Habakkuk 1:4. A crooked closeted hereditary racist Officer of the Most Excellent Order of our Empire of Stolen Affluence - Habakkuk. Sue Gregory (OBE) instructed Richard Hill, and those who nominated, appointed, and instructed Sue Gregory (OBE) paid the salaries of all Judges: Conflict of interest in creeping DPRK.

Your Majesty, vulgar Pharisees' charitable works in exchange for what? Theirs was not a good deal (Matthew 4:9), and it remains a bad deal. They became ultra-righteous and very, very, very, highly civilised, but only after several continuous centuries of MERCILESS RACIST EVIL: The evilest racist terrorism and the greediest economic cannibalism the world will ever know.

Ultra-righteousness without equitable, fair, and just reparation, and the settlement of several centuries of accruing interest, is continuing RACIST FRAUD.

Your Majesty, the defender of only our own faith, the fellow is who He says He is—John 14:6. Based on cogent, irrefutable, and available evidence, the supernatural exists, and it is consistently accessible to those who stand where it can come—John 14:26.

Vulgarly Charitable, Antichrist, and hereditary White supremacist Freemasons are as scared as hell. Theirs' is the evilest Satanic Mumbo Jumbo under God's sun, and trickery and RACIST LIES of members of the vulgarly charitable, Antichrist, and hereditary racist Freemasonry Quasi-Religion—will be unravelled: Mediocre Mafia, New Pharisees, New Good Samaritans (Luke 10:25 -37), New Good Shepherd (John 10: 11–18), New God(deluded and conceited white supremacist bastards awarded themselves the supreme knowledge, and they believe that like Almighty God, they are truly good—Mark 10:18: Integrity, friendship, respect, and charity—all for one, and one for all. Their people are everywhere in Great Britain, and they control almost everything. Defenders of faiths, including the motley assemblies of exotic religions and faiths associated with the 15 Holy Books in the House of Commons, and Dissenters of the Faith—John 14:6, which your Majesty swore before Almighty God to defend.

Your Majesty, vulgarly charitable, Antichrist, and indiscreetly White Supremacist Freemasons are showing NIGERIAN John 14:6 Christians, pepper, in Great Britain. The Judge is watching them—Proverbs 15:3, John 5:22, and Matthew 25: 31-46. The fellow is transparently just – John 5:22, Matthew 25:31 - 46. The nemesis is not extinct, and the fact that it tarries is proof that it will never be some—Habakkuk.

They hate us, and we know. Your Majesty, they unrelentingly persecute our people, your African subjects, for the dark coat that we neither made nor chose, and cannot change, and they steal yields of our Christ granted-talents, and they impede the ascent of our people from the bottomless crater into which their ancestors threw ours, unprovoked, in the African bush, during several continuous centuries of MERCILESS RACIST EVIL: The greediest economic cannibalism and the evilest racist terrorism the world will ever know—Habakkuk. Then, they were insatiably greedy, and greedier than the grave, and like death, they were never satisfied—Habakkuk 2:5.

Based on several decades of very, very, very proximate observations and direct experiences, vulgarly charitable, Antichrist, closeted hereditary White supremacist FREEMASONS are a properly organised gang of EVIL RACIST KILLERS, and they kill hands-off, with the mens rea hidden in the belly of the actus reus, and only our people seem to dying in their unilaterally declared, latent, but very, very, very, potent RACE/RELIGIOUS WAR.

Your Majesty, we are at WAR, and only one side is carrying out all the killing. Like Alexei Navalny, only 47, Richard Bamgboye, Nigerian Medical Practitioner, only 56, and Indian Dentist, Anand Kamath, only 42, did not die naturally, they were KILLED, albeit hands-off, with the mens rea hidden in the belly of the actus reus.

Google: Dr Richard Bamgboye, GP.

Google: Dr Anand Kamath, Dentist.

If pure white supremacist Oxbridge educated rich man's son, Sir, Mr. Justice Haddon-Cave, KC, KBE, alleged Freemason, and all the Closeted Hereditary White Supremacist Freemason Judges in Great Britain, and all the Freemasons at the Masonic Hall, New York City, 71 W 23rd Street #1003, New York, NY 10010, United States, and all the Freemasons at Clifton Masonic Hall, 1496 Van Houten Avenue, Clifton, NJ 07013, United States, and all the Freemasons at The House of the Temple, 1733 16th Street NW Town or City Washington, D.C, United States, and all the Freemasons at the Masonic Lodge, Holly Wood Forever Cemetery, 5970 Santa Monica Boulevard, Los Angeles, CA 90038, United States, and all the 33rd Degree Freemasons at The Masonic Hall, Rising Sun, 1 Mill Road, Wellingborough NN8 1PE, and all the Freemasons at The Acacia Rooms, 27 Rockingham Road, Corby NN17 1AD, and all the Freemasons at Hotspur Lodge №1626, Fern Avenue Masonic Hall, 75–83 Fern Ave, Jesmond, Newcastle upon Tyne NE2 2RA, and all the Freemasons at Kings College School Lodge, Southside Common, London SW19 4TT, and all the members of the Bedfordshire Masonic Centre, the Keep, Bedford Road, Kempston, MK42 8AH, and all the members of Freemasons' Hall, Sheaf Close, Northampton NN5 7UL, and all the members of Towcester Masonic Centre, Northampton Road, Towcester, NN12 6LD, Northamptonshire, and all the 33rd Degree Freemasons (Scottish Rite) at Freemasons' Hall, 96 George Street, Edinburgh EH2 3DH, and all the 33rd

Degree Freemasons (Scottish Rite) at the Provincial Lodge of Glasgow, 54 Berkeley Street, Glasgow G3 7DS, all the 33rd Degree Masons (Scottish Rite), at the Mother Temple, the Grand Masonic Lodge, 60 Great Queen St, London WC2B 5AZ, could disprove the truth, which is that AI recklessly and incompetently lied on record (immortal mendacity), and if they could disprove the truth, which is that Bedford's District Judge Paul Robert Ayers, >70, a Mason, and the Senior Vice President of the Association of Her Majesty's District Judges, 3, St Paul's Square, MK 401SQ, maliciously lied or he was recklessly confused when he explicitly stated that the name of the Defendant on the approved Judgement is the name of the Defendant in the hearings before the approved Judgement, and Senior Judge, albeit England's Class further maliciously lied or he was pathologically recklessly confused (ALZHEIMER'S DISEASE), when he explicitly stated that the NIGERIAN, from shithole Africa, was invited to, and took part in a hearing at Bedford County Court, May House, 29, Goldington Road, Bedford, MK40 3NN, on Monday, 1st July 2013, and if they could disprove the truth, which is that pure White Victoria Harrison, NHS Consultant, Northamptonshire PCT, unrelentingly lied under implied oath and/or record, or she was pathologically confused (Alzheimer's disease), and if they could disprove the truth, which is that which is that OXFORD, ENGLAND: NHS/GDCD/MPS/BDA, Pure White British Soldier, Territorial Defence, Stephanie Twidale (TD), unrelentingly lied under oath—Habakkuk 1:4, and if they could disprove the truth, which is that Pure White Kevin Atkinson, dentist, Scottish Kev, Sterling Kev, Morcott Parish Councillor, alleged Freemason, and England's Class Scottish Postgraduate Tutor, Oxford, unrelentingly LIED under oath- Habakkuk 1:4, and if they could disprove the truth, which is that GDC/NHS, Freemason, Brother, Richard William Hill (NHS Postgraduate Tutor), fabricated reports and unrelentingly lied under oath—Habakkuk 1:4, a very, very, dishonest white man, a closeted hereditary white supremacist NHS Postgraduate Tutor of our Empire of Stolen Affluence—Habakkuk, they will confirm the belief of all Freemasons in the world, which is that very, very, Charitable, Antichrist Freemasonry Quasi-Religion (Mediocre Mafia, New Pharisees, New Good Samaritans (Luke 10: 25–37), New Good Shepherd (John 10: 11- 18), New God (conceited and deluded White Supremacist bastards believe that only they and Almighty God are truly good – Mark 10:18), Defenders of Faiths, including all the motley assemblies of exotic faiths and religions associated with the 15 Holy Books in the House of Commons, and Dissenters of the Faith—John 14:6) is not an intellectually flawed SATANIC MUMBO JUMBO—centuries-old closeted hereditary white supremacists' scam, and they will confirm the belief of Dissenters of the Faith (John 14:6), which is that reasoning and vision have finite boundaries, and if reasoning and vision have finite boundaries, the fellow must have LIED, in the Council, before Romans and Jews, when He, purportedly, disclosed pictures His unbounded painted, and He must have also lied when He audaciously stated that He was Divinely Extra-ordinarily Exceptional—John 14:6. If the fellow told Jews and Romans the truth—in the Council, we are all FORKED, as His Knights attack all Kings and Queens simultaneously, and only Queens can escape, and everything that is not aligned with the exceptionalism of the fellow (John 14:6)—is irreversibly doomed and heading straight for the ROCK.

"It does no harm to throw the occasional man overboard, but it does not do much good if you are steering full speed ahead for the rocks." Sir Ian Gilmour (1926–2007).

District Judge Ayers, a Negro's Encounters: Some White ...Amazon UK. https://www.amazon.co.uk › Racist-White-Judges-Encou... Buy Racist White Judges: District Judge Ayers, a Negro's Encounters: Some White Judges Are Complicit In Racist Fraud by Ayres, Dr Benjamin Bedford (ISBN: ... £16.30

BEDFORD, ENGLAND: Pure White District Judge Paul Robert Ayers, >70, a Mason, and the Senior Vice President of the Association of Her Majesty's District Judges, 3, St Paul's Square, MK40 1SQ, you studied 5th rate law at poly, you are a semi-illiterate, an incompetent racist liar, and your nomination and constructive appointment by dementing or demented White Supremacist Freemason Lords was not based on progressive, colour-blind, measurable objectivity, and you imply that you are a GENIUS, why?

Great Britain is great only because she is very rich (the sixth largest economy on earth). Prior to SLAVERY, there was only subsistence feudal agriculture.

"Agriculture not only gives riches to a nation, but the only one she can call her own." Dr Samuel Johnson (1709–1784).

"Affluence is not a birth right." Lord Cameron.

BEDFORD, ENGLAND: Pure White District Judge Paul Robert Ayers, >70, a Mason, and the Senior Vice President of the Association of Her Majesty's District Judges, 3, St Paul's Square, MK40 1SQ, based on cogent, irrefutable, and available evidence, our own money, Nigeria (oil/gas), is by far more relevant to the economic survival of all your own pure White children than LUTON. Based on cogent, irrefutable, and available evidence, the pure White ancestors of your pure White mother and father were THIEVES and owners of stolen children of poor people, including the pure Black African ancestors of our impure Black Duchess, Meghan Markle (43% Nigerian), and her impure children (<100% White). Facts are sacred, and they cannot be overstated.

"Find the truth and tell it." Harold Pinter (1930 – 2008).

OYINBO OMO OLE: An ignorant ultra-righteous descendant of THIEVES and owners of stolen children of poor people—Habakkuk. Then, very, very, very, greedy racist bastards carried and sold millions of stolen children of poor people, now THIEVES steal our own Africa's natural resources.

"How Europe underdeveloped Africa." Dr Walter Rodney (1942 -1980).

SUBSTITUTION IS FRAUDULENT EMANCIPATION: "Moderation is a virtue only among those who are thought to have found alternatives." Dr Henry Kissinger (1923–2023).

BEDFORD, ENGLAND: Pure White District Judge Paul Robert Ayers, >70, a Mason, and the Senior Vice President of the Association of Her Majesty's District Judges, 3, St Paul's Square, MK40 1SQ, based on cogent, irrefutable, and available evidence, it is plainly deductible that it is absolutely impossible for your Christ-granted talents and yields of the very, very, very, luxuriant land on which your own pure White mother and father were born to sustain your very, very, very, high standard of living. The pure White ancestors of your pure White mother and father were THIEVES and owners of stolen children of poor people, including the pure Black African ancestors of our impure Black Duchess, Meghan Markle (43% Nigerian), and her impure children (<100% White).

"Meghan Markle was the victim of explicit and obnoxious racial hatred." John Bercow, a former speaker

"They may not have been well written from a grammatical point of view but I am confident I had not forgotten any of the facts." Geraint Evans, alleged Rotarian (Freemasonry without voodoo or occultists' rituals), England's Class Welsh Postgraduate Tutor, Oxford, Dentist Rowtree Dental Care, NN4 0NY, and the spouse of wrinkled, wilted, and very ugly Sue, uglier than the Dalit, Suella Braverman (libido killers). His pure White skin concealed his impure dark black brain: Archie is impure (<100% White).

OUR OWN NIGERIA: SHELL'S DOCILE CASH COW SINCE 1956: A very, very, very, bellyful, crooked, and functional semi-illiterate pure White Welsh imbecile, Geraint Evans, whose pure White Welsh mother and father have never seen crude oil, and whose pure White Welsh ancestors, including the pure White Welsh ancestors of Aneurin Bevan (1897 – 1960), were fed like battery hens with yields of stolen children of poor people, including the pure Black African ancestors of the impure (<100% White) niece and nephew of the Prince of Wales, was our England's Class Welsh Postgraduate Tutor, Oxford.

Ignorant descendants of THIEVES and owners of stolen children of poor people, including the pure Black African ancestors of our impure Black Duchess, Meghan Markle (43% Nigerian), and her impure children (<100% White), know how to deal with self-educated Nigerians, from shithole Africa, but they don't know how to repair crooked scatter heads of their functional semi-illiterate hereditary racist pure White kindred – Habakkuk 1:4.

BEDFORD, ENGLAND: Pure White District Judge Paul Robert Ayers, >70, a Mason, and the Senior Vice President of the Association of Her Majesty's District Judges, 3, St Paul's Square, MK40 1SQ, it is not the truth that daily dialogues with a pure White Welsh imbecile, Geraint Evans, alleged Rotarian (Freemasonry without voodoo or occultists' rituals), England's Class Welsh Postgraduate Tutor, Oxford, Dentist Rowtree Dental Care, NN4 0NY, and the spouse of wrinkled, wilted, and very ugly Sue, uglier than the Dalit, Suella Braverman (libido killers), and his type, in a County Court, is a proper job, which is worthwhile, and manly.

John, castrate or sterilise all imbecile Postgraduate Tutors in Great Britain, there are loads of them.

Sheep unnaturally shepherd sheep. Shepherds know that sheep are morons, but sheep do not know that their shepherds are morons too.

"Mediocrity weighing mediocrity in the balance, and incompetence applauding its brother………" Wilde (1854–1900).

"An urgent need for depopulation." John Kerry

WEAKENING OF THE COMMON GENETIC POOL: Part of the resultant effects of several continuous centuries of stealing and Slavery is that a Welsh imbecile, Geraint Evans, alleged Rotarian (Freemasonry without voodoo or occultists' rituals), Dentist Rowtree Dental Care, NN4 0NY, and the spouse of wrinkled, wilted, and very ugly Sue, uglier than the Dalit, Suella Braverman (libido killers) was our Postgraduate Tutor, Oxford. Then, no one went to the Valleys, including Nick Griffin's Llanerfyl Powys, and those who left never went back, hence the weakening of the common genetic pool in Wales.

"The land of my fathers, and my fathers can have it." Dylan Thomas (1914–1953).

Then, in the valleys, including in Nick Griffin's Llanerfyl Powys, there were scores of thousands of white sheep and people, and all the White sheep but not all the people were incestuously conceived, and all the white sheep but not all the people were excessively stupid.

"There is no sin except stupidity." Wilde (1854–1900).

**ONE:** Cambridge University Educated Rich Man's Son, Sir, Mr. Justice Haddon-Cave, KC, which part of our own Royal Courts of Justice, Strand, London WC2A 2LL, did the pure White ancestors of your own pure White mother and father buy, or which part of the Grand Cathedral preceded SLAVERY: The building or its chattels? You are a LEECH. The pure White ancestors of your own pure White mother and father were THIEVES and owners of stolen children of poor people, including the pure Black African ancestors of our impure Black Duchess, Meghan Markle (43% Nigeria), and her impure children (<100% White). You are worthy only because you are pure White and England is very, very, very, rich: The sixth largest economy on earth).

Pure White Rich Man's Son, let me tell you, it is absolutely impossible for your Christ-granted talents and yields of the land of which you were born to sustain your very, very, very, high standard of living. Unlike Putin's Russia, there are no oil wells or gas fields in Bedfordshire, and where your own pure White mother and father were born, and the very, very, very, highly luxuriant soil of Bishop's Stortford yields only FOOD. Bishop's Stortford's Cecil Rhodes (1853–1902), was a HEREDITARY RACIST, very, very, very, greedy, pure White bastard, and an ARMED PROFESSIONAL THIEF—Habakkuk.

"We shall deal with the racist bastards when we get out of prison." Comrade Robert Mugabe (1924 – 2019).

On December 18, 1995, only a week before Christmas, the Nigerian, from shithole Africa, was admitted onto the Bedfordshire NHS Dentist List.

On January 08, 1996, the Nigerian from shithole Africa, started work at 21, Grove Place, Bedford, and the first owned Dental Surgery, in Bedford, since before the Big Bang.

Only after about two weeks of starting work at 21, Grove Place, Richard Hill visited the Nigerian, from shithole Africa, on January 22, 1996, and made some recommendations, and about the structure of the practice and decorations. The Nigerian, from shithole Africa, promptly and fully, acceded to his recommendations, and absolutely everything else was a NEGROPHOBIC, and blatant RACIAL HATRED, and incompetent RACIST LIES—Habakkuk.

"All sections of UK society are institutionally racist." Sir Bernard Hogan-Howe, KBE.

NHS, PCT, GDC, and the Judiciary are parts of UK society.

"The European knows and he does not know. On the level of reflection, a Negro is a Negro, but in the unconscious, there is a firmly fixed image of Nigger-savage." Dr Frantz Fanon (1925–1961).

"The colour bar was crude and cruel. The reasoning bar is spineless cowardice." Ngozi Ekweremadu

"There is a Nigg*r is there. If he touches me, I'll slap his face. You never know with them. He must have great big hands, and besides he's sure to be rough." Dr Frantz Fanon (1925–1961).

HEREDITARY, UNEDUCATED, AND INTELLIGENT NEGROPHOBIA: They criminally subjugate colour-blind objectivity, and they propagate brainless and baseless several centuries-old unspoken myth that the universally acknowledged irrefutably superior skin that the very, very, very, fortunate wearer neither made nor chose is only wonder of our world.

"The white man is the devil." Mohammed Ali (1942–1980).

Based on several decades of very, very, very, proximate observations and direct experiences, a White woman is not only a devil (Jezebel), but she is also a THIEF, and she is crazy—Habakkuk 1:4.

OXFORD, ENGLAND: GDC/NHS/BDA/MPS, British Soldier, Stephanie Twidale (TD), unrelentingly lied under oath—Habakkuk 1:4.

Our very, very, very, dishonest British Soldier. Our crooked closeted hereditary RACIST, a hired GDC/NHS Negrophobic Perjurer.

NEGROPHOBIC PERJURY CONCEALS PERSECUTORY NEGROPHOBIA.

An ignorant ultra-righteous descendant of THIEVES and owners of stolen children of poor people, including the pure Black African ancestors of Kamala Harris—Habakkuk.

Having FAILED in practice, loads did, the British Soldier, Stephanie Twidale (TD), parked her liability at the public till, a very, very, very, cushy salaried job.

Those who FAILED in practice inspected those who didn't.

"She who could, did. She who could not, inspected those thrived where she FAILED.' George Bernard Shaw paraphrased.

Based on very, very, very, proximate observations and direct experiences, weapon of the pure White privileged dullard (predominantly but not exclusively pure White), the direct descendant of the FATHER OF RACIST LIES (John 8:44, John 10:10), is the MOTHER OF RACIST LIES, and her power is the certainty that all Judges would be pure White, and her hope is that all Judges would be pure White bastards too.

"Colour prejudice is nothing more than the unreasoning hatred of one race for another, the contempt of the stronger and richer peoples for those considered inferior to themselves, and the bitter resentment of those who are those whose are kept in subjection and are so frequently insulted. As colour is the most obvious outward manifestation of race, it has been made a criterion by which men are judged, irrespective of their Social and Educational attainment." Dr Frantz Fanon.

Cambridge University Educated Rich Man's Son, Sir, Mr. Justice Haddon-Cave, KC, KBE, let me tell you, reasoning and vision do not have finite boundaries, and the supernatural exists, and it is consistently accessible to those who stand where it can come—John 14:26. The fellow is who He says He is—John 14:6.

"Jesus is the bedrock of my faith." HM (1926 -2022).

The mind that the Nigerian, from shithole Africa, did not choose is finer the LEGAL SYSTEM you serve, as no part of it is good, not even one—Psalm 53, and he has the power to use cogent facts and irrefutable evidence to irreversibly destroy you and it—Habakkuk 1:4.

BEDFORD, ENGLAND: GDC/NHS, Sue Gregory (OBE), alleged Rotarian (Freemasonry without voodoo or occultists' rituals), unrelentingly lied under implied oath— Habakkuk 1:4. A very, very, very, dishonest pure White cougar. A crooked closeted hereditary RACIST Officer of the Most Excellent Order of our Empire of Stolen Affluence—Habakkuk.

Irish Catholic Joseph, President Joe Biden and President Zelensky want all Ukrainians to be part of our very, very, very, HIGHLY CIVILISED, and super-enlightened free world where a very, very, very, crooked hereditary racist pure White woman, Sue Gregory (OBE), unrelentingly lied under implied oath, with audacity, as her own kindred oversaw the administration of their indiscreetly institutionally RACIST LEGAL SYSTEM, but President Putin doesn't, so he used overwhelming extreme violence to covert Avdiivka from bricks to rubble.

**TWO:** Unbeknownst to the Nigerian, from shithole Africa, on August 15, 2006, only a few months after the PCT came into being, a British Soldier (Territorial Defence) contacted a NHS Manager, Mr John Hooper, and asked to review previous reports of visits to the first ever and only Black owned Dental Surgery, in Bedford, since the Big Bang. Three weeks later, on September 06, 2006, Richard Hill released two reports of visits to the surgery of the Nigerian, from shithole Africa: The report of the visit July 22, 2004, and the report of the follow up visit of undisclosed date, and they had what they needed to FU*K the Nigg*r-savage.

'The only good Nigg*r is a dead Nigg*r.'

A Negro was born GUILTY.

Then, a Negro who was seduced by a White Woman, and succumbed to temptation, was castrated.

In Great Britain, if a white woman made an allegation against a Negro—to her own kindred, the Police Force or the Judiciary, the NEGRO is automatically guilty.

On May 30, 2007, Ms Rachael Bishop, Senior NHS Nurse, a patient of the Negro, wrote a letter of complaint, which she sent to the NHS, and later the GDC.

Unbeknownst to the Nigerian, from shithole Africa, on May 30, 2007, three separate incompetent NHS fabrications were live, valid, and accessible to hereditary racist pure bastards (predominantly but not exclusively pure White):

The maliciously and incompetently fabricated NHS report of July 22, 2004.

The fabricated follow-up NHS report of undisclosed date.

The fabricated email address, which the dishonest creator, Mrs Charlotte Dowling (Goodson), NHS Manager, expectedly never employed.

BEDFORDSHIRE, ENGLAND: Mrs Charlotte Dowling (Goodson), unrelentingly lied under oath and/or record — Habakkuk 1:4.

A very, very, very, dishonest pure White cougar.

A crooked closeted hereditary RACIST poly-educated NHS manager.

In the Interim Order Committee Hearing of the GDC, at 37, Wimpole Street, W1G 8DQ, on September 24, 2007, GDC's Counsel stated that there was an adverse report of NHS visit to the surgery of the Nigerian, from shithole Africa, in 2003. GDC lied or was confused, and the Nigerian, from shithole Africa, had never seen the report. Based on cogent, irrefutable, and available evidence, the 2003 report was an incompetent retrospective fabrication by the NHS. At the GDC Interim Order Committee on September 24, 2007, four NHS incompetent RACIST fabrications were live, valid, and accessible to pure White people: The retrospectively fabricated NHS report of July 22, 2004, the retrospectively fabricated NHS follow up report of undisclosed date, the incompetently fabricated Email address, which, expectedly, the creator never employed, and the incompetently created Termination

Statement, of July 30, 2007, which was ladened with blatant RACIST LIES—Habakkuk 1:4.

GDC/NHS: Newcastle Dentist, Shiv Pabary, MBE, JP, a mere Dalit, and the archetypal Indian GDC Committee Chairman, unrelentingly lied under oath and/or on record (Habakkuk 1:4), and he further lied when he implied that he did not know that Richard Hill (NHS) fabricated reports and unrelentingly lied under oath—Habakkuk 1:4. Facts are sacred, and they cannot be overstated.

If Newcastle Dentist, Shiv Pabary, MBE, JP, a mere Dalit, and the archetypal Indian GDC Committee Chairman, who unrelentingly lied under oath and/or on record (Habakkuk 1:4), could disprove the truth, which is that Freemason, Brother Richard William Hill, our Senior NHS Postgraduate Tutor, Oxford, fabricated reports and unrelentingly lied under oath (Negrophobic Perjury concealed Persecutory Negrophobia), he will confirm the belief of scores of millions of Britons, which is that it is UNTRUE that the average Briton is a bloody fool.

"England: About thirty million, mostly fools." Thomas Carlyle (1795–1881).

"The best argument against democracy is a-five-minute conversation with the average voter." Sir Winston Churchill (1874–1965), unapologetic White Supremacist 33rd Degree Freemason, (Scottish Rite).

"Pardon Him Theodotus: He's a barbarian and thinks the customs of his tribe and Island are the laws of nature." George Bernard Shaw (1856–1950).

They are very shallow and narrow, so they do not know that they are incompetent racist liars.

Dr Anand Kamath was threatened with reportage to the GDC; he was shallow, so he killed himself leaving a wife and three children. In pursuance of being the inheritors of heaven, the hands-off killers of Anand will protect his wife and children.

The lioness eats the deer, and fake maternal instinct causes it to protect its Bambi until it's big enough to be eaten, often, other carnivores eat the Bambi before it grows.

"To disagree with three—fourths of the British public on all points is one of the first elements of sanity, one of the deepest consolations in all moments of spiritual doubt." Wilde (1854–1900).

"Find the truth and tell it." Harold Pinter (1930–2008).

The NHS report of 2003 was disclosed to the Nigerian, from shithole Africa, almost six years after it was allegedly created, and the Mediocre GDC seemed too dull to discern the absurdity in the glaringly retrospectively fabricated NHS report, and found against the Nigerian, from shithole Africa, in relation to the brainlessly retrospectively fabricated concerns—no COSSH and no risk assessment.

Brainless nonsense.

Google: Mediocre GDC.

Based on cogent, irrefutable, and available evidence, Shiv Pabary, MBE, JP, alleged Rotarian (Freemasonry without voodoo and/or occultists' rituals), a mere Dalit, and the archetypal Indian GDC Committee Chairman LIED or he was pathologically confused when he implied that he did not discern the absurdity of the 2003 report of Richard Hill, who dishonestly created the reports of July 22, 2004.

OUR OWN MONEY. OUR OWN NIGERIA: SHELL'S DOCILE CASH COW SINCE 1956. Unlike Putin's Russia, there are no oil wells or gas fields in Freemasons' Kempston and where the pure White mother and father of Bedford's District Judge were born. Then, very, very, very, greedy hereditary racist pure White bastards carried and sold millions of stolen children of poor people, including the pure Black African ancestors of our impure Black Duchess, Meghan Markle (43% Nigerian), and her impure children (<100% White), now very, very, very, greedy THIEVES steal our own natural resources from our own Africa. "How Europe undeveloped Africa." Dr Walter Rodney (1942–1980). SUBSTITUTION IS FRAUDULENT EMANCIPATION. "Moderation is a virtue only among those who are thought to have found alternatives." Dr Henry Kissinger (1923–2023).

A brainless racist pure White bastard.

The only evidence of his very, very, very, HIGH IQ is the stolen affluence that his thoroughly wretched ancestors crossed the English Channels, not that long ago, without luggage or decent shoes, to latch onto

Our own Nigerian babies with huge oil wells and gas fields near their huts in our own NIGERIA, a very, very, very, bellyful, physically and/or mentally wonky Indian whose father and mother have never seen CRUDE OIL, thrives in

GREAT BRITAIN. Which part of our own shithole AFRICA is great?

"The best opportunity of developing academically and emotional." Bedford's District Judge Paul Robert Ayers, >70, a Mason, and the Senior Vice President of the Association of Her Majesty's District Judges, 3, St Paul's Square MK40 1SQ.

SHOCKING! "Why, that is, because, dearest, you are a dunce." Dr Samuel Johnson (1709 - 1784).

A MORON UNASHAMEDLY FUNCTIONAL SEMI-ILLITERATE FREEMASON.

A brainless pure White bastard. Only his universally acknowledged irrefutably superior skin colour and Almighty God are truly good—Mark 10:18, and he neither made nor chose it, and he will be considerably diminished as a human being without it, and he knows it.

WHITE PRIVILEGE: His pure White skin concealed his impure dark black brain.

His spinal cord seemed to be his highest centre.

BEDFORD, ENGLAND: District Judge Paul Robert Ayers, >70, a Mason, and the Senior Vice President of the Association of Her Majesty's District Judges, which part of our own Grand Cathedral Court, 3, St Paul's Square, MK 401SQ, was not STOLEN, or which part of it is the yield of the Higher IIQs of the pure White ancestors of your own pure White mother and father, or which part of it preceded SLAVERY: The building or its chattels?

29, Goldington Road, MK40 3NN, is a block of flats.

An ignorant ultra-righteous descendant of THIEVES and owners of stolen children of poor people, including the pure Black African ancestors of our impure Black Duchess, Meghan Markle (43% Nigerian), and impure children (<100% White).

Facts are sacred, and they cannot be overstated.

**THREE:** Then, all Judges were PURE WHITE, and most of them were FREEMASONS, and some of them were THICKER than a gross of planks.

BEDFORD, ENGLAND: GDC/NHS. Freemason, Brother Richard Hill fabricated reports and unrelentingly lied under oath—Habakkuk 1:4.

A very, very, very, dishonest pure White man. A crooked, closeted hereditary racist, vulgarly charitable, and Antichrist FREEMASON.

Amazon

https://www.amazon.co.uk/Boris-Johnson-Closeted-Supremacist-A...

Boris Johnson: Why is England... by Ayres, Dr Benjamin Bedford

WEBDistrict Judge Paul Ayers, the Senior Vice President of the Association of Her Majesty's District Judges— proofed and approved Judgement. A CLOSETED RACIST FOOL'S APPROVAL! The report, by the OECD warns; that the UK needs to take significant action to boost the basic skills of the nation's young people. The 460-page study is based on the ... Author: Dr Benjamin Bedford Ayres

OYINBO OMO OLE: IGNORANT ULTRA-RIGHTEOUS DESCENDANTS OF THIEVES AND OWNERS OF STOLEN CHILDREN OF POOR PEOPLE— HABAKKUK.

Based on several decades of very, very, very, proximate observations and direct experiences, their LEGAL SYSTEM is irreparably bastardised, indiscreetly dishonest, unashamedly mediocre, vindictive, potently weaponised, institutionally RACIST, and overseen by members of the vulgarly charitable, Antichrist, and Closeted White Supremacist Vulgarly Charitable Freemasonry Quasi-Religion. Pure White Cougar, Mrs Helen Falcon, MBE, the mind that the Nigerian, from shithole Africa, did not choose is finer than the SYSTEM you served, and he has the power to use cogent facts and irrefutable evidence to irreversibly destroy you and it.

OXFORD, ENGLAND: GDC/NHS, Mrs Helen Falcon, MBE, Member of the GDC Committee (former), a mere dmf, a vulgarly charitable ROTARIAN (Freemasonry without voodoo and/or occultists' rituals), our Postgraduate Dean, Oxford (former), and the spouse of Mr Falcon, unrelentingly lied under oath and/or on record—Habakkuk 1:4.

A very, very, very, dishonest pure White cougar. A crooked closeted hereditary racist Officer of the Most Excellent Order of our Empire of Stolen Affluence-Habakkuk.

Just like our Universe, our Empire did not evolve from NOTHING, then almost everything was actively and deliberately stolen with guns.

It is plainly deductible that the pure White ancestors of the pure White father and mother of Mrs Helen Falcon (MBE), were incompetent RACIST LIARS too, they were

THIEVES and owners of stolen children of poor people, including the pure Black African ancestors of our impure Black Duchess, Meghan Markle (43% Nigerian), and her impure children (<100% White). Facts are sacred, and they cannot be overstated.

"Those who have robbed have also lied." Dr Samuel Johnson.

An ignorant ultra-righteous descendant of THIEVES and owners of stolen children of poor people, including the pure Black African ancestors of Colin Powell (1937–2021).

Medium

https://medium.com/@cole69915/bedford-district-judge-15c060a00...

BEDFORD, DISTRICT JUDGE. If the white man read his approved

WEBAug 8, 2022 · England is a scam Daringtruths— DISTRICT JUDGE AYERS OF ...—Facebook https://pt-br.facebook.com › Daringtruths01 › photos DISTRICT JUDGE AYERS OF BEDFORD COUNTY COURT: A BRAINLESS WHITE ...

**FOUR:** "Negroes are savages, brutes, and illiterates. ......
The Negro is an animal. The Negro is bad. The Negro is mean. The Negro is ugly. Look, a Nigg*r." Dr Frantz Fanon (1925 – 1961)

*******

GDC CHAMBERS, November 21, 2008:

Pure White Andrew Hurst (GDC's barrister, now a Senior Judge, albeit England's Class): I want to take you to 1996 and back to Bedford.

BAMGBELU: Yes.

Pure White Andrew Hurst (GDC's barrister, now a Senior Judge, albeit England's Class): We have heard the evidence from Mr Hill.

BAMGBELU: Yes

Pure White Andrew Hurst (GDC's barrister, now a Senior Judge, albeit England's Class): You have heard him speak about you. You remember him?

BAMGBELU: Yes.

Pure White Andrew Hurst (GDC's barrister, now a Senior Judge, albeit England's Class): And you remember he came to visit you on a number of occasions in 1996, yes?

BAMGBELU: Yes. I think he came to see me about two or three times in '96, yes.

Pure White Andrew Hurst (GDC's barrister, now a Senior Judge, albeit England's Class): It is also right that Mr Hill told you, in July of 1996 certainly, that several complaints had been received about you.

BAMGBELU: In July '96?

Pure White Andrew Hurst (GDC's barrister, now a Senior Judge, albeit England's Class): He told you that.

BAMGBELU: No.

Pure White Andrew Hurst (GDC's barrister, now a Senior Judge, albeit England's Class): Do you accept, first of all, that is what Mr Hill has recorded?

BAMGBELU: I would like to tell you first that

THE LEGAL ASSESSOR (MR DAVID SWINSTEAD): No. Please answer the question.

THE CHAIRMAN (DR SHIV PABARY, MBE, JP): It is important.

Pure White Andrew Hurst (GDC's barrister, now a Senior Judge, albeit England's Class): And it is probably more in your interest to listen to the question.

BAMGBELU: No.

Pure White Andrew Hurst (GDC's barrister, now a Senior Judge, albeit England's Class): Sorry? You do not accept that he has written it down here?

BAMGBELU: No.

Pure White Andrew Hurst (GDC's barrister, now a Senior Judge, albeit England's Class): He has written it down, has he not?

BAMGBELU: These statements were recovered by Mrs Sally Wright.

Pure White Andrew Hurst (GDC's barrister, now a Senior Judge, albeit England's Class): Hold on. Perhaps you misunderstand the question. First of all because the Committee do not have the document we are looking at, all right?

BAMGBELU: Yes.

Pure White Andrew Hurst (GDC's barrister, now a Senior Judge, albeit England's Class): So we can take it in stages. Surely you do agree with me that we are all looking at a piece of paper with 24 April 96 written on it.

BAMGBELU: Yes.

Pure White Andrew Hurst (GDC's barrister, now a Senior Judge, albeit England's Class): That a written complaint has been received, and the key areas of complaint are the rough manner in which the patient was examined and abusive language used by the dentist.

BAMGBELU: Yes.

Pure White Andrew Hurst (GDC's barrister, now a Senior Judge, albeit England's Class): So you accept, first of all, that Mr Hill has made a record to that effect. I am not asking you whether it is true or not. I am not asking you where it has come from or anything else at the moment. I would just like you to confirm, for the sake of record, that that is what is written down on Mr Hill's record.

DAVID MORRIS (MPS barrister): Just before the witness answers, can I have a word with my learned friend? (Pause)

Pure White Andrew Hurst (GDC's barrister, now a Senior Judge, albeit England's Class): Mr Morris has made a very helpful suggestion. Let us leave Mr Hill out of it for the moment as to who may have compiled the document, all right?

BAMGBELU: Yes.

Pure White Andrew Hurst (GDC's barrister, now a Senior Judge, albeit England's Class): Somebody at the PCT has created a record which says 24 April 1996: 'Rough manner in which patient examined, abusive language used by the dentist.'

BAMGBELU: Yes.

Pure White Andrew Hurst (GDC's barrister, now a Senior Judge, albeit England's Class): You accept that someone has made that record.

BAMGBELU: Yes.

Pure White Andrew Hurst (GDC's barrister, now a Senior Judge, albeit England's Class): I am sorry if I misled you.

*********

Ipse dixit: It is said, therefore it is the truth.

It is not the truth that everything members of the brainlessly and baselessly self-awarded SUPERIOR RACE say about NIGERIANS, from shithole Africa, is the truth.

"There is a Nigg*r in there, if he touches me, I'll slap his face. You never know with them. He must have great big hands and besides, he is sure to be rough." Dr Frantz Fanon (1925–1961).

Big black hands are the visible evidence of invisible HUGE BLACK ROCKS, Nigg*rs' fertility tools.

SEXUAL ENVY: The Nigg*rs penis is his sword.

"The Negro is viewed as a penis symbol …… Is the lynching of the Negro not a sexual revenge? We know how much sexuality there is in all cruelties, tortures, and beatings." Dr Frantz Fanon.

THE TYRANNY PURE WHITE MAJORITY: ENDURING RESIDUES OF SLAVERY, COLONISATION, EXPLOITATION, RACIAL HATRED, AND PERSECUTION.

"The white man is the devil." Elijah Mohammed (1897–1975).

Based on several decades of very, very, very, proximate observations and direct experiences, a White man is not only a devil, but he is also a THIEF, and he is thoroughly CRAZY.

BEDFORD, ENGLAND: GDC/NHS, Freemason, Brother, Richard William Hill, Senior NHS Postgraduate Tutor, Bedfordshire, fabricated reports and unrelentingly lied under oath—Habakkuk 1:4.

A very, very, very, dishonest pure White man. A crooked closeted hereditary racist FREEMASON.

Facts are sacred, and they cannot be overstated.

OYINBO OLE: THIEVES—HABAKKUK.

GDC: 37, Wimpole Street, W1G 8DQ, protects the British public, and regulates dentists.

"This and no other is the root from which a tyrant springs, when he first appears he is a protector." Plato.

Based on cogent, irrefutable, and available evidence, GDC Manager (casework)Poly-educated (not Russell Second-Class Alternative Education—Proverbs 17:16, Pure White Jonathan Martin, 1 Colmore Row, Birmingham B4 6AA, unrelentingly lied under oath and/or on record—Habakkuk 1:4.

The pure White ancestors of the pure White mother and father of Jonathan Martin were incompetent RACIST LIARS too, they were THIEVES and owners of stolen children of poor people, including the pure Black African ancestors of Dr Martin Luther King (1929–1968).

Dr Martin Luther King and Christ were killed only because they spoke, and they were not punished for speaking, they were KILLED solely to prevent them from speaking.

MATTHEW 14: John was jailed only because he spoke, and the intolerant LUNATIC JEW removed his head solely to permanently prevent him from speaking.

Our own NIGERIAN BABIES with huge oil wells and fields near their huts eat only 1.5/day in our NIGERIA, very, very, very, bellyful poly-educated Jonathan Martin, a mere poly-educated plebeian pure White bastard whose pure White mother and father have never seen CRUDE OIL, and whose pure White ancestors, including the pure White Welsh ancestors of Aneurin Bevan (1897–1960), were fed like battery hens with yields of stolen children of poor people, including the pure Black African ancestors of our impure Black Duchess, Meghan Markle (43% Nigerian), and her impure children (<100% White), was GDC Manager (casework), in our own Great Britain. Which part of our shithole AFRICA is great?

Aneurin Bevan's NHS was preceded SLAVERY—and paid for it.

Facts are sacred, and they cannot be overstated.

Jonathan Martin, GDC Manager (casework): Which part of 37, Wimpole Street, London, W1G 8DQ, and 1 Colmore Row, B4 6AA, did the pure White ancestors of your own pure White mother and father buy, or which part of it preceded SLAVERY: The building or its chattels?

An ignorant ultra-righteous descendant of THIEVES and owners of stolen children of poor people.

BIRMINGHAM, 1968: When unapologetic White supremacist 33rd Degree FREEMASON (Scottish Rite), Enoch Powell (1912–1998) gave his speech, there were Rivers of Blood in our own Biafra. Then, very, very, very, greedy, pure White THIEVES

Google: Biafra Mark II

BEDFORD, ENGLAND: District Judge Paul Robert Ayers, >70, a Mason, and the Senior Vice President of the Association of Her Majesty's District Judges, 3, St Paul's

Square, MK40 1SQ, the very, very, very, highly luxuriant land on which your own pure White mother and father were born yields only FOOD. You are verifiably a functional semi-illiterate. You are relatively very, very, very, rich, and you DISHONESTLY implied that you did not know that the pure White ancestors of your own pure White father and mother were THIEVES and owners of stolen children of poor people, including the pure Black African ancestors of Meghan Markle (43% Nigerian), and her impure children (<100% White).

An extremely nasty opportunist racist pure White bastard was granted the platform to display hereditary prejudice, nastier than Yevgeny Prigozhin (1961 – 2023).

BEDFORD, ENGLAND: GDC/NHS, Sue Gregory (OBE), alleged Rotarian (Freemasonry without rituals and/voodoo) unrelentingly lied under implied oath and/or on record.

Based on several decades of very, very, very, proximate observations and direct experiences, there is no law in their country. Their Law is, essentially, what vulgarly charitable, hereditary White Supremacist, and Antichrist FREEMASONS want.

Based on several decades of very, very, very, proximate observations and direct experiences, they are psychologically and intellectually insecure, and like LUNATIC JIHADISTS, they are dogmatically impervious to other views.

**FIVE:** New Herod (Matthew 2:16, 14): Like Putin, Kim, MBS, and babies, they expect EVERYONE to love them unconditionally, and they expect all NIGERIANS, from shithole Africa, to see our common world only from the perspective of members of the brainlessly and baselessly self-awarded SUPERIOR RACE (unipolarity), and they expect all our people to write and/or say only what they love to hear: Creeping DPRK.

The ancestors of Kim did not kidnap and imprison a whole people—overnight, they did gradually, and the basic right to disclose pictures painted by free minds was the first to be withdrawn.

"Freedom of expression is a basic right." Lady Hale.

Medium

https://medium.com/@cole69915/poly-educated-racist-rubbish-226...

Poly-educated racist rubbish.—Medium

WEBMar 15, 2023 · It is plainly deductible that the white father and mother of Bedford's District Judge Paul Robert Ayers, > 70, a Mason, and the Senior Vice President of the Association of Her Majesty's ...

On 21.11.2008, Andrew Hurst, white British Barrister took the black African back to 1996 (13 years prior) in pursuant of corroborating the allegations by a racist, but exceedingly dull white British senior NHS nurse.

Members of the White British tribe expressed understanding when dim, racist, and white British Stephanie Twidale did not remember 2007 in 2008.

Members of the White British tribe expressed understanding when dishonest and racist, white British Richard Hill did not remember 2006 in 2008.

Members of the White British tribe expressed understanding when very, very, very, dim, half-wit, and hereditary racist, white British Kevin Atkinson did not remember 2007 in 2008.

The pure White imbecile barrister, now our Senior Judge, albeit England's Class, expected the only black man in the process to remember 1996 in 2008, with only the allegations that were made against him, 13 years prior; he was intellectually disoriented and mentally very dull, and expectedly so, but he was also a closet, RACIST THUG.

WHITE PRIVILEGE GUARDS WHITE SUPREMACY: One rule for whites and another rule for blacks, and that is not new news!

"White supremacy is real, and it needs to be shattered." Dr Cornel West

Based on several decades of very, very, very, proximate observations and direct experiences, only very, very, very, stupid NIGERIANS, from shithole Africa, expect members of the brainlessly and baselessly self-awarded SUPERIOR RACE to voluntary relinquish centuries-old advantageous positions in exchange for NOTHING, and only stupider NIGERIANS, from shithole Africa, expect closeted hereditary White supremacist Freemason Judges to measure their own 'culturally advanced' kindred with the same yardstick they use to measure mere NIGERIANS, from shithole Africa, and only the stupidest among NIGERIANS, from shithole Africa, expect demons to cast out demons—Matthew 12:27.

Pure White Andrew Hurst (GDC's barrister, now a Senior Judge, albeit England's Class), read Richard Hill's statement of 23.09.2008, concerning 1996 reports, and he did not understand it. Had he, he would have practised proper law in Strand, and he would not have parked his liability at the till of dentists' money, at 37, Wimpole Street, W1G 8DQ, and he would have realised that Richard Hill did not give Mr Bamgbelu reports, but sent him separate letters about recommendations based on his visits.

The pure White imbecile Barrister of our Empire of Stolen Affluence—Habakkuk, Pure White Andrew Hurst (GDC's barrister, now a Senior Judge, albeit England's Class), believed what Poly-educated pure White bastards at Mills and Reeve Solicitors, Birmingham, not too far from GDC Offices, at 1 Colmore Square, B4 6AA, and led by a mere for Legal Office boy, plebeian, Kevin Duce, who gained adult-education Law Degree at Poly: Not Russell Group Second Class Alternative Education—Proverbs 17:16.

Pure White Andrew Hurst, the white British barrister, reasoned like a semiliterate Gypsy, and he expressed his reasoning like a Semi-illiterate Pakistani. Gypsies, white Britons and Pakistanis are in the lowest third on the list of those meeting academic targets at age, as implied by Centre Forum.

'Do you accept, first of all, that is what Mr Hill has recorded?' Andrew Hurst, white British barrister, at the GDC chambers, on 21.11.2008

When the fu*k are we going to have second of all from the pure White opportunist racist imbecile Barrister?

Andrew Hurst, white British barrister, could read, but he had not fully acquired the consistent capacity to understand all he had read, which was consistent with the observations of Wilde, George Bernard Shaw, Sir Winston Churchill, and the findings of OECD and CentreForum.org.

The functional unashamedly semi illiterate, imbecile barrister of our Empire of Stolen Affluence read the statement below and believed that Richard Hill was the one who created it. Had Almighty God blessed him with the intellect of a yellow man (Chinese—first on the list of those meeting educational targets at age 16), he would have thought differently.

'Memorandum from Mrs Sally Wright to Richard Hill copied to John Swain.

'Pure White Gypsies, Brown Pakistanis, Andrew Hurst's tribe (White Britons) were in the lowest third of those meeting educational targets at age 16—Gypsy's class. Wilde, George Bernard Shaw, Sir Winston Churchill, Quentin Crisp, OECD and Centre Forum, corroborated one another and implied that the average so-called white Briton, the most populous ethnic group, and the best sample of Britons, was a moron.

'To disagree with three-fourths of the British public on all points is one of the first elements of sanity, one of the deepest consolations in all moments of spiritual doubt.' Wilde (1854–1900).

'Pardon him Theodotus: He is a barbarian and thinks that the customs of his tribe and Island are the laws of nature.' George Bernard Shaw (1856–1950).

'The best argument against democracy is a five-minute conversation with the average voter.' Sir Winston Churchill (1874–1965), an unapologetic White supremacist 33rd Degree Freemason (Scottish Rite).

FREEMASONS: Vulgarly Charitable, Antichrist, and White Supremacist bastards do Voodoo and/or occultists' rituals, and they lie that they don't lie—Psalm 144.

One man one vote democracy is a White supremacists' scam, as human beings are not equally created by Almighty God.

'The English think that incompetence is the same thing as sincerity.' Quentin Crisp (1908–1999).

FAILING SCHOOLS AND A BATTLE FOR BRITAIN: This was the day the British education establishment's 50-year betrayal of the Nation's children lay starkly exposed in all its ignominy. After testing 166,000 people in 24 education systems, the Organisation for Economic Cooperation and Development (OECD) finds that England's young adults are amongst the least literate and numerate in the industrialised world (Paul Dacre, Daily Mail, 09.01.2013).

At age 5, the white British majority tribe was third on the list of those hitting educational targets, and only about a decade later, at age 16, the white British majority tribe had descended to 13th on the list of those hitting educational targets. If the pattern of decline continues, it should be time to objectively assess whether the finest filtration of the white British majority tribe was the best available, as the cleverest and most selfless must be our shepherds, irrespective of shade and tribe.

**SIX:** "The near absence of women and Black, Asian and minority ethnic judges in the senior judiciary, is no longer tolerable. It undermines the democratic legitimacy of our legal system." Sir Geoffrey Bindman, KC and Karon Monaghan, KC, 2014.

*******

GDC CHAMBERS, NOVEMBER 21, 2008:

ANDREW HURST (GDC's barrister): Do you accept, first of all, that is what Mr Hill has recorded?

BAMGBELU: I would like to tell you first that.

THE LEGAL ASSESSOR (MR DAVID SWINSTEAD): No. Please answer the question.

BAMGBELU: 'Fu*k you, two-head acromegaly pure White bastard', the Nigerian, from shithole Africa, exclaimed, but inaudibly.

THE CHAIRMAN (DR SHIV PABARY, MBE, JP): It is important.

BAMGBELU: 'Of course, it is, imbecile Indian', the NIGERIAN, from shithole Africa, exclaimed, but only, internally.

The re-enactment of a Kangaroo Court in Colonial Africa: The enduring residues the brutal rule of the RACIST, and very, very, very, very, European Christian occupiers.

Then, the very, very, very, greedy, and oppressive RACIST pure White bastard were greedier than the grave, and like death, they were never satisfied.

Then, they find a very, very, very dull Indian, preferably a cow worshipper, only cows with milk, and not bulls with no milk, and they adorn him with very, very, very, high titles, and he becomes Freemasons' Zombie Private Soldier.

"Truth, Sir, is a cow that will yield such people no more milk, so they are gone to milk the bull." Dr Samuel Johnson

"I think I will ask our legal adviser for any advice he may have. My view is that there are six or seven of us here who had the admission down, but we cannot find it in the transcript and there is wordings that imply that there was, but it is not in black and white….." Dr Shiv Pabary, Member of the Most Excellent Order of our Empire (MBE), Justice of Peace (JP), the archetypal Indian GDC Committee Chairman, and an alleged vulgarly charitable ROTARIAN (Freemasonry with occultists' rituals and/or voodoo).

"Yes, Sir, it does her honour, but it would do nobody else honour. I have indeed not read it all. But when I take up the end of a web, and find a packthread, I do not expect, by looking further, to find embroidery." Dr Samuel Johnson

Based on cogent, irrefutable, and available evidence, Dr Shiv Pabary, Member of the Most Excellent Order of Empire (MBE), Justice of Peace (JP), the archetypal Indian GDC Committee Chairman, and an alleged vulgarly charitable ROTARIAN (Freemasonry with occultists' rituals and/or voodoo), maliciously lied, or he was recklessly intellectually disorientated and mentally imbalanced (recklessness is malice), when he stated, "I think will ask our legal adviser for any advice he may have. My view is that there are six or seven of us here who had the admission down, but we cannot find it in the transcript...."

"Lies are told all the time." Sir Michael Havers (1923–1992).

Based on cogent, irrefutable, and available evidence, the crooked, hereditary racist Indian, a near-perfect imitation upper-class Englishman maliciously LIED, or he was recklessly confused, when he stated that there were six of them there, and he further LIED when he implied that the NIGERIAN, from shithole Africa, bribed the pure White transcript writer not to record what the allegedly six, too many, RACIST BASTARDS wrote down.

Based on cogent, irrefutable, and available evidence, in our own Great Britain, there was cash for Questions, and in our own NIGERIA, in shithole Africa, there was cash for Judgement. If those who made laws demanded and accepted BRIBES, it is plainly deductible that those merely interpreted laws made by those who demanded and accepted bribes—may demand and accept BRIBES too.

**SEVEN:** Had it been in our own Nigeria, in our own shithole Africa, there wouldn't have been any doubt in the mind of the NIGERIAN, from shithole Africa—that Dr Shiv Pabary, Member of the Most Excellent Order of Empire (MBE), Justice of Peace (JP), the archetypal Indian GDC Committee Chairman, and an alleged vulgarly charitable ROTARIAN (Freemasonry with occultists' rituals and/or voodoo), had been 'settled', and the Indian (Uncle Tom), recklessly immortalised incompetent mendacity for eternity.

Based on cogent, irrefutable, and available evidence, Dr Shiv Pabary, Member of the Most Excellent Order of Empire (MBE), Justice of Peace (JP), the archetypal Indian GDC Committee Chairman, and an alleged vulgarly charitable ROTARIAN (Freemasonry with occultists' rituals and/or voodoo), maliciously lied, or he was recklessly intellectually disorientated and mentally imbalanced (recklessness is malice), when he stated, there is wordings that imply that there was, but it is not in black and white….."

Like Rastafarians, some Indians smoke weed.

Dr Shiv Pabary, Member of the Most Excellent Order of Empire (MBE), Justice of Peace (JP), the archetypal Indian GDC Committee Chairman, and an alleged vulgarly charitable ROTARIAN (Freemasonry with occultists' rituals and/or voodoo), was so mentally wonky, had he been BLACK, he might have been sectioned under the Mental Health Act. According to information that is available in the public domain, his brother is wonky too. Their Indian mother and father could be related. Sex-

Machine, Charles Darwin (1809–1882) married his first cousin, and expectedly, their children, not all, were wonky. Albert Einstein (1879–1955) married his first cousin, and all their children were so wonky, they all died in utero.

"….there is wordings that imply that there was, but it is not in black and white….." Shiv Pabary, JP, and the archetypal Indian GDC Committee Chairman.

Shiv Pabary, JP, and the archetypal Indian GDC Committee Chairman, let me tell you, if there were wordings that implied that there was, and they were not in BLACK and WHITE, they might have been written in Red, Gold, Black, and Green.

Pabary, it was weed. Shiv, it was cheap impure ganja, at 37, Wimpole Street, London, W1G 8DQ.

"Rally round the flag. Rally round the Red,
 Gold, Black, and Green. Marcus say Sir Marcus say
 Red for the blood that flowed like the river. Marcus say, Sir Marcus says, Green for the land Africa. Marcus says yellow for the gold that they stole. Marcus says Black for the people it was looted from. They took us away. Required from us a song …….How can we sing in a strange land." Steel Pulse

Ignorant ultra-righteous descendants of THIEVES and owners of stolen children of poor people, including the pure Black African ancestors of our impure Black Duchess, Meghan Markle (43% Nigerian), and her impure children (<100% White).

\*\*\*\*\*\*\*\*

Mr David Swinstead and Dr Shiv Pabary (MBE, JP) seemed prejudiced, and they allowed prior predilection to override objective reasoning.

The RACIST bastards did not realise that it was impossible to answer stupid questions, even if they were 'second of all'.

Based on several decades of very, very, very, proximate observations and direct experiences, their legal system is sclerotic and seemingly tailor made for privileged dullards.

In order to sell mediocrity and confusions for value, some people join unelected (illegal, parallel power), not merit based, and a closeted RACIST satanic network.

Integrity, friendship, respect, and charity (all for one, and for all): They wear vulgar charitable as a cloak of deceit, and they swear by the name of Almighty God never to tell lies, but they lie that they do not lie (Songs of David 144 paraphrased).

BEDFORD, ENGLAND: District Judge Paul Robert Ayers, >70, a Mason, and the Senior Vice President of the Association of Her Majesty's District Judges, 3, St Paul's Square, MK40 1SQ, the mind that the NIGERIAN, from shithole Africa, did not choose is finer than the indiscreetly White Supremacist Legal System that you served, and he has the POWER to use cogent facts and irrefutable evidence to irreversibly DESTROY you and it. You are LEECH, and the pure White ancestors of your own pure White father and mother were THIEVES and owners of stolen children of poor people, including the pure Black African ancestors of the impure (<100% White) great grandchildren of the Duke of Edinburgh, of blessed memory, Prince Phillip (1921–2021).

Philippians 1:21: Phillip was a 33rd Degree Freemason (Scottish Rite).

Facts are sacred.

"The truth allows no choice." Dr Samuel Johnson

BEDFORD, ENGLAND: GDC/NHS, Sue Gregory (OBE), alleged vulgarly charitable ROTARIAN (Freemasonry without occultists' rituals and/or voodoo), unrelentingly lied under implied oath and/or record—Habakkuk 1:4.

A very, very, very, dishonest pure White cougar. A crooked closeted hereditary RACIST Officer of the Most Excellent Order of our Empire of Stolen Affluence— Habakkuk.

Medium

https://medium.com/@yinkabamgbelu45/bedford-district-judge-our ...

BEDFORD: District Judge, our own Money, NIGERIA (oil/gas) is

WEBNov 3, 2021 · Bedford. District Judge Ayers, 08/06/21. Justice, 08/06/21. Her Honour Judge Gargan. Daringtruths—His Honour Judge Perusko studied at Poly… | Facebook https://en-gb.facebook.com

They hate us, and we know.

**EIGHT:** "The white man is the devil." Brother Mohammed Ali (1942–2016).

Based on very, very, very, proximate observations and direct experiences, a White woman is not only a devil (JEZEBEL), but she is also a THIEF, and she is thoroughly crazy.

OXFORD, ENGLAND: NHS/GDC, Mrs Helen Falcon (MBE), Member of the GDC Committee (former), a mere dmf, a vulgarly charitable Rotarian (Freemasonry without voodoo or occultists' rituals), our Postgraduate Dean, Oxford (former), and the spouse of Mr Falcon, unrelentingly lied under oath and/or on record— Habakkuk 1:4.

A very, very, very, dishonest pure White cougar. Based on very, very, very, proximate observations and direct experiences, on November 25, 2009, Mrs Helen Falcon (MBE), looked like a dirty grandma who regularly visited the Gambia to sit on black rocks, in exchange for harder currency.

Dishonesty is the most important hallmark of HEREDITARY RACIAL HATRED, and it is considerably more common than ordinarily realised.

"White supremacy is real, and it needs to be shattered." Dr Cornel West.

A crooked closeted hereditary racist descendant of THIEVES and owners of stolen children of poor people, including the pure Black African ancestors of our impure

Black Duchess, Meghan Markle (43% Nigerian), and her impure children (<100% White).

It is plainly deductible that all dishonest Members of the Most Excellent Order of our Empire of Stolen Affluence are RACISTS.

Just like our universe, our Empire did not evolve from NOTHING, then, almost everything was actively and deliberately stolen with GUNS.

"Those who have robbed have also lied." Dr Samuel Johnson (1709- 1784).

Like vulgarly charitable, Antichrist, and hereditary White supremacist members of the occultist Freemasonry Quasi-Religion (Mediocre Mafia, New Pharisees, New Good Samaritans (Luke 10:25–37), New Good Shepherd (John 10:11–18), New God (Freemasons believe that only they and Almighty God are truly good—Mark 10:18: Integrity, friendship, respect, and charity—all for one, and one for all), defenders of faiths, including all the motley assemblies of exotic religions and faiths associated with the 15 Holy Books in the House of Commons, and Dissenters of the Faith—John 14:6, some vulgarly charitable Rotarians (auxiliary Freemasons), like Mrs Helen Falcon (MBE), tell incompetent RACIST LIES under oath and/or on record (Negrophobic Perjury) because they are not deterred by His Justice (John 5:22, Matthew 25:31–46), and why should they, when they do not believe in the exceptionalism of the fellow—John 14:6.

Based on cogent, irrefutable, and available evidence, our Pure White Member is not Excellent because she is, verifiably, a very, very, very, hardened RACIST PURE WHITE CRIMINAL—Habakkuk 1:4.

Based on several decades of very, very, very, proximate observations and direct experiences, the weapon of the pure White privileged dullard (predominantly but not exclusively pure White), the direct descendant of the father of lies (John 8:44, John 10:10) is the mother of all racist lies, and her power is the certainty that all Judges will be PURE WHITE, and her hope is that all Judges will be racist pure White bastards too – Habakkuk 1:4.

"Sometimes people don't want to hear the truth because they don't want their illusions destroyed." Friedrich Nietzsche (1844–1900).

Mrs Helen Falcon (MBE), England's Class Postgraduate Dean, Oxford, nominated, appointed, and instructed Geraint Evans, England's Class Welsh Postgraduate Tutor, Oxford, and those who nominated, appointed, and instructed Mrs Helen (MBE), paid the salaries of all Judges: Conflict of interest in creeping DPRK.

"A government that robs Peter to pay Paul can always depend on the support of Paul." George Bernard Shaw (1856–1950).

WALES, A QUASI-PROVINCE OF ENGLAND: It is plainly deductible that England is the natural resource of Wales. If Wales were to be detached from England at the River Severn, in Monmouthshire, and other boundary regions, she will become poorer than Albania, but not Ukraine.

NHS/GDC: Based on cogent, irrefutable, and available evidence, Geraint Evans, alleged Rotarian (Freemasonry without voodoo or occultists' rituals), England's Class Welsh Postgraduate Tutor, Oxford, Dentist Rowtree Dental Care, NN4 0NY, and the spouse of wrinkled, wilted, and very ugly Sue, uglier than the Dalit, Suella Braverman (libido killers), unrelentingly lied under implied oath and/or on record—Habakkuk 1:4.

A very, very, very, dishonest pure White Welshman. A crooked closeted hereditary racist descendant of pure White Welsh THIEVES and owners of stolen children of poor people, including the pure Black African ancestors of the impure (<100% White) niece and nephew of the Prince of Wales. Dishonesty is the Engine that drives RACIAL HATRED. Racial hatred is not a myth, and it is not extinct, and it is considerably more common than ordinarily realised.

"The earth contains no race of human beings so totally vile and worthless as the Welsh. ......." Walter Savage Landor (1775–1864).

Medium

https://medium.com/@cole69915/bedford-district-judge-why-is-engla...

BEDFORD: District Judge, why is England very, very rich?

WEBAug 14, 2022 · A YouTube video accuses District Judge Ayers of Bedford County Court of being a racist and a hypocrite who uses his position to discriminate against black people …

BEDFORD, ENGLAND: Pure White District Judge Paul Robert Ayers, >70, a Mason, and the Senior Vice President of the Association of Her Majesty's District Judges, 3, St Paul's Square, MK40 1SQ, which part of our own Grand Cathedral County Court did the pure White ancestors of your own pure White father and mother buy, or which part of the truly magnificent building preceded SLAVERY: The building or its chattels? Then, in Great Britain, yields of merciless racist evil, stolen lives of children of poor people, including the pure Black African ancestors of our impure Black Duchess, Meghan Markle (43% Nigerian), and her impure children (<100% White), were used to build GREAT COURTS, and yields of stealing and slavery were used to pay the wages of FREEMASON JUDGES who sent those who stole money to GREAT PRISONS built with yields of stolen children of poor people—Habakkuk.

Facebook

https://www.facebook.com/Daringtruths01/posts/33995582501687…

Daringtruths—BEDFORD: District Judge, your ancestors,.

WEBNov 10, 2021 · District Judge Paul Ayers, Bedford. A fool's approval. Only fools approve mediocrity and immortalise it for eternity! If District Judge Paul Ayers of Bedford County Court, 3 St Paul's Square Bedford, MK40 9 DN, read the Judgement that he approved, he must be a fool. If he didn't, he must have lied as he implied that he did.

Mrs Helen Falcon (MBE), Member of the GDC Committee (former), a mere dmf, a vulgarly charitable Rotarian (Freemasonry without voodoo or occultists' rituals), our Postgraduate Dean, Oxford (former), and the spouse of Mr Falcon, Geraint Evans, alleged Rotarian (Freemasonry without voodoo or occultists' rituals), England's Class Welsh Postgraduate Tutor, Oxford, Dentist Rowtree Dental Care, NN4 0NY, and the spouse of wrinkled, wilted, and very ugly Sue, uglier than the Dalit, Suella Braverman (libido killers), and/or their type killed the Indian Dentist, only 42, albeit hands-off, with the mens rea hidden in the belly of the actus reus.

Google: Dr Anand Kamath, Dentist.

BEDFORD, ENGLAND: Pure White District Judge Paul Robert Ayers, >70, a Mason, and the Senior Vice President of the Association of Her Majesty's District Judges, 3, St Paul's Square, MK40 1SQ, it is plainly deductible that it is absolutely impossible for your talent and yields of the land on which your own pure white mother and father were born to sustain your high standard of living. The pure White ancestors of your pure White mother and father were THIEVES and owners of stolen children of poor people, including pure Black African ancestors of Meghan Markle (43% Nigerian), our impure Black Duchess, and her impure children (<100% White). Based on several decades of very, very, very, proximate observations and direct experiences, there is no law in their goddamned country, as their law is what members of the vulgarly charitable,

Antichrist, and hereditary White Supremacist Freemasonry Quasi-Religion want: Mediocre Mafia, New Pharisees, New Good Samaritans (Luke 10: 25–37), New Good Shepherd (John 10: 11–18), New God (conceited and closeted hereditary racist bastards seem to believe that only they and Almighty God are truly good—Mark 10:18), Defenders of Faiths, including the motley assemblies of exotic religions and faiths associated with the 15 Holy Books in the House of Commons, and Dissenters of the Faith—John 14:6. They hate us, and we know.

They love SUPERIORITY, their baseless and brainless inviolable birth right, but they hate Freedom of Expression because they don't want their mentally gentler children to know the truth, which is that the centuries-old unspoken myth that intellect is related to the universally acknowledged irrefutably superior skin colour that the very, very, very, fortunate wearer neither made nor chose is the mother of all RACIST SCAMS.

Based on several decades of very, very, very, proximate observations and direct experiences, they hate us more than their ancestors hated ours. It is logical to expect their children to hate ours more than they hate us.

They are, purportedly, very, very, very, highly civilised, and super-enlightened, and they do everything, absolutely everything LEGALLY (rules-based procedures, precedent, and statute etcetera), but including HEREDITARY RACIAL HATRED and FRAUD—Habakkuk 1:4.

Their people are everywhere, and they control almost everything in their country. Integrity, friendship, respect, and charity: All for one, and for all. They are not the only creation of Almighty God, and they are not immortal, and the universally acknowledged irrefutably SUPERIOR SKIN COLOUR that the very, very, very, fortunate wearer neither made nor chose is not the only wonder of our world, and they will be considerably diminished as human beings without it, and they know it: WHITE PRIVILEGE.

Facebook

https://www.facebook.com/Daringtruths01/posts/theyre-extremely-...

Daringtruths—They're extremely nasty racist white…—Facebook

WEBMay 22, 2023 · 3 Apr 2021—District Judge Paul Ayers of Bedford County Court, the Senior Vice President of the Association of Her Majesty's District Judges. GDC: Helen Falcon (MBE) lied on record. OUR DISHONEST RACIST. OUR WHITE WOMAN. BEDFORD, ENGLAND: Our semi-illiterate Freemason District Judge of our Empire of STOLEN AFFLUENCE. Our …

**NINE:** BEDFORD, ENGLAND: Pure White District Judge, Paul Robert Ayers, >70, a Mason, and the Senior Vice President of the Association of Her Majesty's District Judges, 3, St Paul's Square, MK40 1SQ, let me tell you, the most important part of the matter is MONEY, and it is not the yield of your land or talent. The pure White ancestors of your own pure White father and mother were THIEVES and owners of stolen children of poor people. Our own money, NIGERIA (oil/gas) is by far more relevant to the economic survival of all your own White children, your pure White father, your pure White mother, and your pure White spouse than Freemasons' Kempston. Unlike Putin's Russia, there are no oil wells or gas fields in Freemasons' Northampton and where your own pure White mother and father were born. The pure White ancestors of your own pure White father and mother were THIEVES and owners of stolen children of poor people, including the pure Black African ancestors of our impure Black Duchess, Meghan Markle (43% Nigerian), and her impure children (<100% White). "Sometimes people don't want to hear the truth because they don't want their illusions destroyed." Friedrich Nietzsche (1844 – 1900).

Which one of our putrid tubes did our Born-Again Christian tell Pure White District Judge Paul Robert Ayers, >70, a Mason, and the Senior Vice President of the Association of Her Majesty's District Judges, 3, St Paul's Square, MK40 1SQ, and Freemasons at Brickhill Baptist Church she used to work for £0.5M?

2 Thessalonians 3:6–10: Then, all Judges were pure White, and most of them were FREEMASONS, and they sent their

daughters to universities to gain qualifications so that they can eat their own FOOD, but also to use their putrid tubes to ensnare fellow university students who would pay them for pleasurable intermittent insertions: Quasi-Hoes.

They found two holes, hypothyroidism, and RELIGIOUS PSYCHOSIS, and they deceived our Born-Christian that the destruction of the father of her children was in her best interest, and they knew that she was too dull to realise that the principal objective of hereditary RACIST BASTARDS was to destroy her children.

"England is like a prostitute who, having sold her body all her life, decides to close her business, and then tells everybody that she wants to be chaste, and protect her flesh, as if it were jade." He Manzi.

Based on several decades of very, very, very, proximate observations and direct experiences, they are extremely wicked hereditary White supremacist bastards, and they hate us, and we know, and they hate our children more, and we know that too.

Based on several decades of very, very, very, proximate observations and direct experiences, they hate our children more, but they don't know.

They are like a lioness, in the African bush, who killed and ate a baboon, and after being very, very, very, bellyful, there was a maternal hormonal gush, which caused her to be protective of the baby baboon whose mother the bastard had ate, and when the baby baboon grew bigger, the carnivorous bastard ate it too.

RACIAL HATRED should not be a personal sin if it is genetic.

We are all who we are, the inheritors of our inheritances, genes of our individual ancestors.

BEDFORD, ENGLAND: Pure White District Judge Paul Robert Ayers, >70, a Mason, and the Senior Vice President of the Association of Her Majesty's District Judges, 3, St Paul's Square, MK40 1SQ, let me tell you, the pure White ancestors of your own pure White father and mother were THIEVES and owners of stolen children of poor people, including the pure Black African ancestors of our impure Black Duchess, Meghan Markle (43% Nigerian), and her impure children (<100% White). Based on cogent, irrefutable, and available evidence, the entire foundation of your civilisation is MERCILESS RACIAL HATRED and FRAUD - Habakkuk.

The mind that the NIGERIAN, from shithole Africa, did not choose, is finer than the legal system you serve, and he does not believe in any part of it, as no part of it is good, not even one – Psalm 53, and he has the POWER to use cogent facts and irrefutable evidence to irreversibly destroy you and it.

Reasoning and vision are unbounded, and the supernatural exists, and it is consistently accessible to those who stand where it can come—John 14:26.

The fellow is who He says He is—John 14:6, and alignment to His exceptionalism of the Divine Good Shepherd (John 10:11–18) is not optional, as survival, and continuing propagation desires it, more than any other thing.

Not by choice, but only through the unsolicited kindness of the fellow, the NIGERIAN, from shithole Africa, is a FOETUS, as what he can vividly see is clearer than dreams, visions, and prophecies.

"The white man is the devil." Elijah Mohammed (1897–1975).

Based on several decades of very, very, very, proximate observations and direct experiences, a White man is not only a DEVIL, but he is also a THIEF, and he is thoroughly crazy.

OYINBO OMO OLE: THIEVES-HABAKKUK.

Then, racist bastards carried and sold millions of stolen children of poor people, now THIEVES steal our own natural resources from our own AFRICA.

SCOTLAND, A MERE QUASI-PROVINCE OF ENGLAND: NHS/GDC, Kevin Atkinson, Scottish Kev, Sterling Kev, Dentist Little Glasgow(Corby), England's Class Scottish Postgraduate Tutor, Oxford, Councillor Morcott Parish, alleged Rotarian (Freemasonry without voodoo and/or occultists' rituals), and the spouse of ugly Annie, uglier than the Dalit, Suella Braverman (libido killers), unrelentingly lied under oath—Habakkuk 1:4.

The pure White Scottish ancestors of the pure White Scottish mother and father of pure White Kevin Atkinson were incompetent RACIST LIARS too, they were THIEVES and owners of stolen children of poor people.

A very, very, very, DISHONEST pure White Scotchman. A crooked closeted hereditary racist England's Class Scottish Postgraduate Tutor, Oxford.

They hate us, and we know.

"As hard hearted as a Scot of Scotland." English saying.

An ignorant hereditary racist pure White bastard.

If you did not know that Scots are very, very, very, interested in other people's money, it is the conclusive proof that you couldn't see them.

"Scots, Jews, and counterfeit money will be encountered all over the world." German saying.

It is not the truth that all Scots are shifty.

Maxwell is a Scottish name.

Robert Maxwell (1923–1991) was a very, very, very, shifty bastard, and a THIEF.

"There are few more impressive sights in the world than a Scotsman on the make." Sir J.M. Barrie (1860 – 1937).

Then, they used extreme violence to compel stolen children of poor people to pick cotton and cut cane, and every day, except SUNDAYS, when they were forced to sing 'stand up, stand up, for Jesus', in a strange land.

'How can we sing in a strange land.' Steel Pulse.

And the pure White bastards fu*ked (raped) stolen Black daughters, and beautiful Black sons, of poor people, every night, including SUNDAY NIGHTS, and after several continuous centuries of merciless racist evil, they became ultra-righteous, very, very, very, highly civilised, and super-enlightened.

Properly rehearsed ultra-righteousness, and deceptively schooled civilised decorum were preceded by several continuous centuries of merciless RACIST EVIL: The greediest economic cannibalism and the evilest RACIST TERRORISM the world will ever know.

The EVIL RACIST BASTARDS were greedier than the grave, and like death, they were never satisfied— Habakkuk 2:5.

They hate us, and we know. If you did not know that TRUTH, it is proof that you couldn't see them.

\*\*\*\*\*\*\*\*\*\*

Case No: 2YL06820

Bedford County Court

May House

29 Goldington Road

Bedford

MK40 3NN

Monday, 1st July 2013

B E F O R E:

DISTRICT JUDGE AYERS

DOBERN PROPERTY LIMITED

(Claimants)

v.

DR. ABIODUN OLA BAMGBELU

(Defendant)

Transcript from an Official Court Tape Recording.

Transcript prepared by:

MK Transcribing Services

29 The Concourse, Brunel Business Centre,

Bletchley, Milton Keynes, MK2 2ES

Tel: 01908–640067 Fax: 01908–365958

DX 100031 Bletchley

Official Court Tape Transcribers.

MR. PURKIS appeared on behalf of THE CLAIMANTS.

THE DEFENDANT appeared in PERSON.

JUDGMENT

(As approved)

************

If the hereditary racist pure White bastard, albeit England's Class Senior Judge, Paul Robert Ayers, >70, a Mason, and the Senior Vice President of the Association of Her Majesty's District Judges, 3, St Paul's Square, MK40 1SQ, read his approved Judgement, he was a FOOL, and if he didn't, he lied as he implied that he did – Habakkuk 1:4.

Based on cogent, irrefutable, and available evidence, the pure White ancestors of his pure White father and mother of Bedford's District Judge Paul Robert Ayers, >70, a Mason, and the Senior Vice President of the Association of Her Majesty's District Judges, 3, St Paul's Square, MK40 1SQ, were incompetent RACIST LIARS too, they were THIEVES and owners of stolen children of poor people, including the pure Black African ancestors of our impure Black Duchess, Meghan Markle (43% Nigerian), and impure children (<100% White).

Facts are sacred, and they cannot be overstated.

"The truth allows no choice." Dr Samuel Johnson (1709 – 1784).

Based on cogent, irrefutable, and available evidence, SEXED-UP LEGAL TRANSCRIPTS are not uncommon in the administration of English Law – Habakkuk 1:4.

Google: Incompetent Liars: Some Lawyers.

Google: The Law Paralysed.

No brain. Poor natural resources. Several continuous centuries of stealing and Slavery preceded the HUGE STOLEN TRUST FUND.

"They may not have been well written from a grammatical point of view." Geraint Evan, Our England's Class Welsh Imbecile Postgraduate Tutor, Oxford.

BEDFORD, ENGLAND: District Judge Paul Robert Ayers, >70, a Mason, and the Senior Vice President of the Association of Her Majesty's District Judges, 3, St Paul's

Square, MK40 1SQ, it is not the truth that daily dialogues with IMBECILES, including crooked, and hereditary racist, Pure White Welsh imbecile, Geraint Evans, England's Class Postgraduate Tutor, Oxford, is proper job that is worthwhile and manly.

Two, too many, unashamedly functional semi-illiterate crooked pure White bastards.

"The best opportunity of developing academically and emotional." Pure White Bedford's District Judge Paul Robert Ayers, >70, a Mason, and the Senior Vice President of the Association of Her Majesty's District Judges, 3, St Paul's Square, MK40 1SQ – Proof-read and Approved Judgement.

A brainless racist pure White bastard. The universally acknowledged irrefutably superior skin colour that the Senior Judge, albeit England's Class, neither made nor chose concealed his impure dark black brain.

OUR OWN NIGERIA: SHELL'S DOCILE CASH COW SINCE 1956.

Unlike Putin's Russia, there are no oil wells or gas fields in Freemasons' Northamptonshire and where the pure White mother and father of pure White Bedford's District Judge Paul Robert Ayers, >70, a Mason, and the Senior Vice President of the Association of Her Majesty's District Judges, 3, St Paul's Square, MK40 1SQ, were born.

Our own Nigerian babies with huge oil wells and gas fields near their huts eat only 1.5/day in our own NIGERIA, Pure White Bedford's District Judge Paul Robert Ayers, >70, a

Mason, and the Senior Vice President of the Association of Her Majesty's District Judges, 3, St Paul's Square, MK40 1SQ, a very, very, very, bellyful pure White man, a mere poly-educated former debt-collector Solicitor in NORWICH (5$^{th}$ Rate Partner), whose pure White mother and father have never seen CRUDE OIL, and whose pure White ancestors, including the pure White ancestors of unapologetic White Supremacist 33$^{rd}$ Degree Freemason (Scottish Rite), were fed like battery hens with yields of stolen children of poor people, including the pure Black African ancestors of the impure (<100% White), great grandchildren of the Duke of Edinburgh, of blessed memory, Prince Phillip (1921 – 2021), thrives in GREAT BRITAIN. Which part of our own shithole Africa is great?

Philippians 1:21: Phillip was a 33$^{rd}$ Degree Freemason (Scottish Rite).

Based on several decades of very, very, very, proximate observations and direct experiences, they hate us, and we know.

BEDFORD, ENGLAND: Based on cogent, irrefutable, and available evidence, Pure White District Judge Paul Robert Ayers, >70, a Mason, and the Senior Vice President of the Association of Her Majesty's District Judges, 3, St Paul's Square, MK40 1SQ, maliciously lied or he was pathologically recklessly confused (ALZHEIMER'S DISEASE),when he explicitly stated that the NIGERIAN, from shithole Africa, was invited to, and took part in a hearing at Bedford County Court, May House, 29, Goldington Road, Bedford, MK40 3NN, on Monday, 1st July 2013.

Facts are sacred: 29, Goldington Road, Bedford, MK40 3NN, is block of flats.

Based on cogent, irrefutable, and available evidence, the SENIOR JUDGE, albeit England's Class—lied, and did immortally.

"Lies are told all the time." Sir Michael Havers (1923 - 1992).

The Pure White Senior Judge, albeit England's Class, further lied, under oath, when he stated (implicitly) that the name of the Defendant in the Court hearings before the proof-read and approved Judgement—is the same.

A RACIST DESCENDANT OF THIEVES AND OWNERS OF STOLEN CHILDREN OF POOR PEOPLE—HABAKKUK:

"Those who have robbed have also lied." Dr Samuel Johnson

Based on several decades of very, very, very, proximate observations and direct experiences, theirs is irreparably bastardised, indiscreetly DISHONEST, unashamedly mediocre, vindictive, potently weaponised, and institutionally racist—Habakkuk 1:4.

Dr Richard Dawkins and OECD implied that all the children, grandchildren, and great grandchildren of Bedford's District Judge should be duller than their unashamedly functional semi-illiterate Patriarch.

"Natural selection will not remove ignorance from future generations." Dr Richard Dawkins

"The best opportunity of developing academically and emotional." Pure White Bedford's District Judge Paul Robert Ayers, >70, a Mason, and the Senior Vice President of the Association of Her Majesty's District Judges, 3, St Paul's Square, MK40 1SQ.

"I don't want to talk grammar. I want to talk like a lady." George Bernard Shaw (1856 – 1950).

Facts are sacred, and they cannot be overstated. A brainless racist pure White bastard. His pure White skin concealed his impure dark black brain.

Our imbecile Freemason Senior District Judge of our Empire of STOLEN AFFLUENCE – Habakkuk. His spinal cord seemed to be his highest centre.

"He who joyfully marches to music rank and file has already earned my contempt. He has been given a large brain by mistake, since for him the spinal cord would surely suffice. This disgrace to civilization should be done away with at once. Heroism at command, senseless brutality, deplorable love-of-country stance and all the loathsome nonsense that goes by the name of patriotism, how violently I hate all this, how despicable and ignoble war is; I would rather be torn to shreds than be part of so base an action! It is my conviction that killing under the cloak of war is nothing but an act of murder." Albert Einstein (1879–1955).

Again, based on cogent, irrefutable, and available evidence, It is not the truth that the name of the Defendant on the approved Judgement is the name of the Defendant in the hearings before the approved Judgement—Habakkuk 1:4.

If there are cogent and irrefutable evidence that the pure White ancestors of the pure White mother and father of Bedford's District Judge Paul Robert Ayers, >70, a Mason, and the Senior Vice President of the Association of Her Majesty's District Judges, 3, St Paul's Square, MK40 1SQ, were THIEVES: Extremely nasty, and merciless, racist murderers, nastier than Yevgeny Prigozhin (1961 -2023), industrial-scale professional armed robbers, armed land grabbers, gun runners in the African bush, opium merchants (drug dealers), and owners of stolen children of defenceless poor people, including the pure Black African ancestors of our impure Black Duchess, Meghan Markle (43% Nigerian), and her impure children (>0% Black), it would be very, very, very, naive not to expect RACIAL HATRED complicated by incompetent mendacity to be part of the genetic inheritances of Bedford's District Judge

"Meghan Markle was the victim of explicit and obnoxious racial hatred." John Bercow, a former speaker

Facts are sacred, and they cannot be overstated.

Then, very, very, very, greedy hereditary racist pure White bastards introduced guns to the African bush, and it became possible for an armed imbecile to kill a wiser man, and for a spineless wimp to kill a stronger man, and they artificially fomented wars in the AFRICAN wars in the African bush, and these wars were RACIST SMOKE SCREENS, as they were euphemism for organised industrial-scale theft of children of poor people.

Facebook

https://www.facebook.com/Daringtruths01/posts/35813174386594…

Daringtruths—A semi-illiterate former debt-collector…—Facebook

WEBJan 3, 2022 · District Judge Paul Ayers, Bedford. A fool's approval. Only fools approve mediocrity and immortalise it for eternity! If District Judge Paul Ayers of Bedford County Court, 3 St Paul's Square. GDC: Richard Hill fabricated reports and …

**TEN:** GOOGLE: MEDIOCRE GDC. Jonathan Martin, Case Work Manager GDC, alleged Rotarian (Freemasonry without voodoo and/or occultists' rituals), 37, Wimpole Street, London W1G 8DQ, poly-educated (not Russell Group Second Class Alternative Education—Proverbs 17:16), pure White rubbish, unrelentingly lied under oath and/or on record—Habakkuk 1:4. A very, very, very, DISHONEST pure White man. A crooked closeted hereditary racist descendant of THIEVES and owners of stolen children of defenceless poor people, including the pure Black African ancestors of our impure Black Duchess, Meghan Markle (43% Nigerian), and her impure children (<100% White). "All sections of UK Society are institutionally racist." Sir Bernard Hogan-Howe. GDC is part of UK society.

Jonathan Martin, Case Work Manager GDC, alleged Rotarian (Freemasonry without voodoo and/or rituals), 37 Wimpole Street, London W1G 8DQ, when was the GDC established, and white part of it did the pure White ancestors of your own pure White father and mother buy, or which part of 37 Wimpole Street, London W1G 8DQ and 1 Colmore Square, B4 6AA, preceded Slavery: The buildings or their chattels?

An ignorant descendant of THIEVES and owners of stolen children of defenceless poor people, including the pure Black African ancestors of Kamala Harris.

OXFORD, ENGLAND: GDC/NHS, Mrs Helen Falcon, MBE, Member of GDC Committee (former), a mere dmf, a vulgarly charitable Rotarian (Freemasonry without voodoo and/or rituals), our Postgraduate Dean, Oxford, and the spouse of Mr Falcon, unrelentingly lied under oath and/or on record—Habakkuk 1:4.

A very, very, very, dishonest pure White cougar. A crooked closeted hereditary racist Member of the Most Excellent Order of our Empire of Stolen Affluence—Habakkuk.

Just like our universe, our Empire did not evolve from NOTHING, then almost everything was actively and deliberately stolen with GUNS.

"They may not have been well written from a grammatical point of view but I am confident I have not forgotten any of the facts." Geraint Evans, England's Class Welsh Postgraduate Tutor, Oxford.

Mrs Helen Falcon, MBE, and Member of the GDC Committee (former), appointed and instructed Geraint Evans, and those who appointed and instructed Mrs Helen Falcon, MBE, and Member of GDC Committee, paid the salaries of all Judges.

Conflict of interest in creeping DPRK.

"A government that robs Peter to pay Paul can always depend on the support of Paul." George Bernard Shaw.

BEDFORD, ENGLAND: District Judge Paul Robert Ayers, >70, a Mason, and the Senior Vice President of the Association of Her Majesty's District Judges, 3, St Paul's Square, MK40 1SQ, it is not the truth that daily dialogues with IMBECILES, including Geraint Evans, England's Class Welsh Postgraduate Tutor, Oxford, is a proper job that is worthwhile and manly.

Facts are sacred, and they cannot be overstated.

They know how to deal with NIGERIANS, from shithole Africa, who disagree with members of the brainlessly and baselessly self-awarded SUPERIOR RACE, but they do not know how to repair scatter-heads of their own pure White kindred—Habakkuk 1:4.

Then, when Solicitors and Barristers FAILED in practice, very many did, if they were Freemasons, they became Judges or something else, and if not, they became Politicians or something else. Then, those who could, did, and those who could not, made laws or interpreted laws—Habakkuk 1: 4.

"The best opportunity of developing academically and emotional." Bedford's District Judge Paul Robert Ayers, >70, a Mason, and the Senior Vice President of the Association of Her Majesty's District Judges, 3, St Paul's Square, MK40 1SQ.

A brainless opportunist racist pure White bastard approved what his pure White father and mother spoke, which his poly-educated pure White superiors and supervisors in LUTON authorised.

HHJ Perusko studied law at Poly: Not Russell Group Second Class Alternative—Education—Proverbs 17:16.

Perception is grander than reality.

WHITE PRIVILEGE: Based on several decades of very, very, very, proximate observations and direct experiences, everything, and absolutely everything, is assumed in favour of the universally acknowledged irrefutably superior skin colour that the very, very, very, fortunate wearer neither made nor chose.

They are not the only creation of Almighty God, and their universally acknowledged irrefutably superior skin colour is not the only wonder of our world.

OUR OWN NIGERIA: SHELL'S DOCILE CASH COW SINCE 1956.

GDC was established in 1956.

Bedfordshire Masonic Centre, the Keep, MK42 8AH. Unlike Putin's Russia, there are no oil wells or gas fields in Freemasons' Kempston and where the pure White father and mother of Bedford's District Judge were born.

URANIUM: American and Russian troops are camped next to each other in Niger.

There are no oil wells, gas fields, or uranium mines in Birmingham and where the White mother and father of Enoch Powell (1912–1998) were born, and in 1968, when the one-dimensionally educated White Supremacist Bastard gave his speech, in Birmingham, there were rivers of Blood in crude oil and gas rich BIAFRA.

There are no gold or diamond mines in Bishop's Stortford, and the very, very, very, highly luxuriant soil of Bishop's Stortford yields only FOOD. Bishop's Stortford's Cecil Rhodes (1853–1902) was a very, very, very, greedy racist pure White bastard and a THIEF.

"How Europe underdeveloped Africa." Dr Walter Rodney (1942–1980).

They hate us, and we know. Then, very, very, very, greedy racist bastards carried and sold millions of stolen children of poor people, including the pure Black African ancestors of the impure (<100% White) niece and nephew of the Prince of Wales, now they steal our own natural resources from our own Africa.

"We shall deal with the racist bastards when we get out of prison." Robert Mugabe (1924–2019).

SUBSTITUTION IS FRAUDULENT EMANCIPATION.

"Moderation is a virtue only among those who are thought to have found alternatives." Henry Kissinger (1923–2023).

Our own Nigerians babies with huge oil wells and gas fields near their huts eat only 1.5/day in our own NIGERIA, a very, very, very, bellyful, crooked, and hereditary racist pure White bastard, a mere poly-educated former debt-collector Solicitor in NORWICH (5th Rate Partner)—whose pure White mother and father have never seen crude oil, and whose pure White ancestors, including the pure White ancestors of Aneurin Bevan (1897–1960), were fed like battery hens with yields of stolen children of defenceless poor people, including the pure Black African ancestors of our impure Black Duchess, Meghan Markle (43% Nigerian), and her impure children (<100% White), was our Senior District Judge, in our own Bedford, Great Britain. Which part of our own shithole Africa is great? Slavery preceded Bevan's NHS, and it paid for it.

"Meghan Markle was a victim of explicit and obnoxious racial hatred." John Bercow, a former speaker.

Based on several decades of very, very, very, proximate observations and direct experiences, the pattern of merciless racist evil is the same everywhere in their indiscreetly institutionally racist mediocre country.

"The white man is the devil." Mohammed Ali (1942–2016).

Based on several decades of very, very, very, proximate observations and direct experiences, a White woman is not only a devil (Jezebel), but she is also a THIEF, and she is thoroughly crazy.

OXFORD, ENGLAND: GDC/NHS/BDA/MPS, British Soldier, Territorial Defence, Stephanie Twidale (TD). unrelentingly lied under oath—Habakkuk 1:4.

A very, very, very, dishonest crooked cougar. A crooked closeted hereditary racist British Soldier (Territorial Defence)—Habakkuk.

The USA is NATO, and absolutely everything else is an auxiliary bluff.

President Zelensky and President Joseph Biden want all Ukrainians to be part of our very, very, very, highly civilised, and super-enlightened free world where pure White people, only pure White people, are allowed to fabricate reports and tell incompetent racist lies under oath, but President Putin doesn't, so he used extreme violence to convert Avdiivka from bricks to rubble and stole it.

OYINBO OLE: THIEVES—HABAKKUK.

Poly-educated pure White rubbish, Jonathan Martin, Case Work Manager GDC, alleged Rotarian (Freemasonry without voodoo and/or rituals), 37 Wimpole Street, London W1G 8DQ, let me tell you, reasoning and vision do not have finite boundaries, and the supernatural exists, and it is consistently accessible to those who stand where it can come—John 14:26. The fellow is who He says He is—John 14:6.

"Jesus is the bedrock of my faith." HM (1926–2022).

Jonathan Martin, Case Work Manager GDC, alleged Rotarian (Freemasonry without voodoo and/or rituals), 37 Wimpole Street, London W1G 8DQ, let me tell you, the mind that the Nigerian, from shithole Africa, did not choose is finer than the system you serve, and she does not believe in any part of it, as no part of it is good, not even one – Psalm 53, and she has the power to use cogent facts and irrefutable evidence to irreversibly destroy you and it—Habakkuk.

"He is a typical Englishman, usually violent and always dull." Wilde.

BEDFORD, ENGLAND: GDC/NHS, Sue Gregory, OBE, alleged Rotarian (Freemasonry without voodoo and/or occultists' rituals) unrelentingly lied under implied oath and/on record—Habakkuk 1:4.

A very, very, very, dishonest pure White cougar. A crooked closeted hereditary racist Officer of the Most Excellent Order of our Empire of Stolen Affluence—Habakkuk.

Her type KILLED the Indian dentist, Anand Kamath, only 42, albeit hands-off, with the mens rea hidden in the belly of the actus reus.

Based on several decades of very, very, very, proximate observations and direct experiences, they have only one method of doing RACIST EVIL, and they use it all the time: They criminally attach RACIST EVIL to Nigerians, from shithole Africa, who disagree with members of the brainlessly and baselessly self-awarded SUPERIOR RACE, and they do RACIAL HATRED until it takes hold, and when it does, they instantly revert to LEGALITY, the legality whose entire foundation is RACIAL HATRED and FRAUD—Habakkuk 1:4.

Based on several decades of very, very, very, proximate observations and direct experiences, the weapon of pure White privileged dullard (predominantly but not exclusively pure White), the direct descendant of the father of RACIST LIES (John 8:44, John 10:10), is the mother of RACIST LIES, and their power is the certainty that all Judges would be PURE WHITE, and their hope is that all Judges would be pure White racist bastards too—Habakkuk 1:4.

Based on several decades of very, very, very, proximate observations and direct experiences, deluded and conceited, they brainless and baselessly awarded themselves the supreme knowledge, and they deceive their mentally gentler children and the imbeciles they shepherd that they do everything legally, including RACIAL HATRED and FRAUD: Rules-based procedures, statute, and precedent etcetera.

They are very, very, very, intolerant to other views, and they are brainlessly and baselessly dogmatic (UNIPOLARITY), and they are more impervious to other views than LUNATIC JIHADISTS, and like Putin, Kim, MBS, and Babies, they expect everyone to love them unconditionally, and they expect Africans, from shithole Africa, including NIGERIANS, to see the world from the perspective of members of the self-awarded SUPERIOR RACE, and want all our people to write and/or say only what they love to hear: CREEPING DPRK.

The ancestors of Kim did not kidnap and imprison a whole people overnight, they did overnight, and the basic right to disclose pictures painted by minds driven by God's free air—was the first to be withdrawn.

"Freedom of Expression is a basic right." Lady Hale.

They hate us, and we know. They persecute our people for the dark coat that we neither made nor chose, and cannot change, and they steal yields of Christ Christ-granted talents by criminally constructively annulling our formal education, and they maliciously economically strangulate our people, and they sadistically place insurmountable obstacles before our people, and the impede the ascent of our people from the bottomless crater into which their very, very, very, greedy racist bastard ancestors threw ours, in the AFRICAN BUSH, unprovoked, during several continuous centuries of merciless RACIST EVIL: The evilest racist terrorism and the greediest economic cannibalism the world will ever know—Habakkuk.

Based on several decades of very, very, very, proximate observations and direct experiences, they are extremely wicked, and they are greedier than the grave, and like death, they are never satisfied—Habakkuk 2:5.

They have taken everything, and only life remains, and they possess the power to take that too, they will inevitably do. We shall go, and they must come—2 Samuel 12:23.

"Those have the power to do wrong with impunity seldom wait long for the will." Dr Samuel Johnson.

Sue Gregory OBE instructed Richard Hill, and those who instructed Sue Gregory, Officer of the Most Excellent Order of our Empire of Stolen Affluence paid the wages of all Judges.

They were all Pure White, and homogeneity in the administration of their law is the impregnable secure mask of MERCILESS RACIST EVIL—Habakkuk 1:4.

Based on several decades of very, very, very, proximate observations and direct experiences, the Nigerian, from shithole Africa, saw EVIL in Great Britain, and it is PURE WHITE.

"I have seen EVIL, and it has the face of Mark Fuhrman." Johnnie Cochran (1937–2005).

Only our visible chains are off, and only stupid NIGERIANS, from shithole Africa, expect the direct descendants of the owners and/or exploiters of their direct ancestors to voluntarily relinquish centuries-old advantageous positions in exchange for NOTHING.

"There is no sin except stupidity." Wilde.

Ignorance is bliss.

"The white man was created a devil, to bring chaos upon the earth." 1925–1965.

Medium

https://medium.com/@mluther88983/vindictive-fury-of-a-satanic-wh…

VINDICTIVE FURY OF A SATANIC WHITE FREEMASONS' NETWORK: RACIST MASON JUDGES

WEBNov 23, 2023 · WebSir Winston Churchill Based on accessible information, it is the absolute truth that District Judge Ayers of Bedford County Court in Bedfordshire, England, …

**ELEVEN:** Based on several decades of very, very, very, proximate observations and direct experiences, loads of Judges are Freemasons, but not all Judges are hereditary White Supremacist crooked bastards. The administration of English Law is irreparably bastardised, indiscreetly DISHONEST, unashamedly mediocre, VINDICTIVE, potently weaponised, institutionally RACIST, and overseen by MASONS: Mediocre Mafia, New Pharisees, New Good Samaritans (Luke 10: 25–37), New Good Shepherd (John 10: 11–18), New God (conceited and deluded vulgarly charitable Antichrist White supremacist self-awarded ultra-righteous bastards believe that they and Almighty God are truly good—Mark 10:18; integrity, friendship, respect, and charity: all for one, and one for all, Defenders of Faiths, including the motley assemblies of exotic religions and faiths associated with the 15 Holy Books in the House of Commons, and Dissenters of the Faith—John 14:6.

Then, all Judges were PURE WHITE, and most of them were FREEMASONS, and some of them were thicker than a gross of planks.

"They may not have been well written from a grammatical point of view but I am confident I had not forgotten any of the facts." Pure White Welsh imbecile, Geraint Evans, England's Class Welsh Postgraduate Tutor, Oxford, and alleged Rotarian (Freemasonry without voodoo and/or occultists' rituals).

BEDFORD, ENGLAND: District Judge Paul Robert Ayers, >70, a Mason, and the Senior Vice President of the Association of Her Majesty's District Judges, 3, St Paul's Square, MK 401SQ, it is not the truth that daily dialogues with pure White imbeciles (predominantly but not exclusively pure White), including Pure White Welsh imbecile, Geraint Evans, England's Class Welsh Postgraduate Tutor, Oxford, and alleged Rotarian (Freemasonry without voodoo and/or occultists' rituals), and his type, is a proper job that is worthwhile and manly. WALES, A MERE QUASI-PROVINCE OF ENGLAND: GDC/NHS, Geraint Evans, Dentist Rowtree Dental Care, NN4 0NY, unrelentingly lied under implied oath— Habakkuk 1:4. A very, very, very, DISHONEST pure White Welshman. Our crooked closeted hereditary RACIST Welsh Imbecile, our Postgraduate Tutor, Oxford. "The earth contains no race of human beings so totally vile and worthless as the Welsh……." Walter Savage Landor (1775–1864).

Medium

https://medium.com/@cole69915/russians-and-ukrainians-are-busil…

Russians and Ukrainians are busily destroying themselves and

WEBAug 14, 2022 · District Judge Ayers, Bedford. Freemasons teach members secret handshakes, not grammar. GDC: Richard Hill fabricated reports and unrelentingly lied under oath. GDC: Kevin Atkinson (NHS ...

GDC Lied. Andrew Hurst, Now A Judge, Albeit England's Class … Amazon.it. https://www.amazon.it › Lied-And…·Translate this page. White skin and stolen trust fund, before slavery, what? When it becomes mandatory for all Judges to publish handwritten legal and factual basis of their. HHJ Persusko studied law at Poly: Not Russell Group Second Class Alternative Education—Proverbs 17:16. It is universally acknowledged and irrefutable that skin colour that they neither made nor chose is SUPERIOR to ours, but it is plainly deductible that their intellects are not, and to balance the unbalanced, hereditary White Supremacist bastards steal yields of FOREIGNERS' Christ-granted talents. BEDFORD, ENGLAND: GDC/NHS, Sue Gregory (OBE), alleged Rotarian (Freemasonry without occultists' rituals and/or voodoo), unrelentingly lied under implied oath and/or on record—Habakkuk 1:4. A very, very, very, DISHONEST pure White cougar. A crooked closeted hereditary RACIST Officer of the Most Excellent Order of our Empire of Stolen Affluence -Habakkuk.

OYINBO OMO OLE: THIEVES – HABAKKUK.

CHRIST KILLERS (Matthew 27: 32–56): Then, very, very, very, greedy bastards killed the Good Shepherd (John 10: 11- 18), and now the direct descendants of Christ killers rob His sheep. Romans were here for several centuries, from 55BC. Then, greedy bastards carried and sold millions of stolen children of poor people, now they steal our own natural resources from our own AFRICA. The Carrying Trade is IMMORTAL. The Judge is watching them—John 5:22, Matthew 25:31–46, and Proverbs 15:3.

Equitable, fair, and just REPARATION pends, and several continuous centuries of unpaid interest accrue.

Ase gbe kan ko si la be orun, ase pamo paapa kosi loju OLODUMARE.

"The report, by the OECD, warns that the UK needs to take significant action to boost the basic skills of the nation's young people. The 460-page study is based on the first-ever survey of the literacy, numeracy and problem-solving at work skills of 16 to 65-year-olds in 24 countries, with almost 9,000 people taking part in England and Northern Ireland to make up the UK results. The findings showed that England and Northern Ireland have some of the highest proportions of adults scoring no higher than Level 1 in literacy and numeracy—the lowest level on the OECD's scale. This suggests that their skills in the basics are no better than that of a 10-year-old." OECD.

AN IMBECILE: AN ADULT WITH THE BASIC SKILLS OF A CHILD.

Then, those who administered the law, including Judges, were recruited from a pool of IMBECILES.

Apart from creating cushy salaried jobs for Solicitors and Barristers who couldn't hack it in the very competitive real world (quasi-communism), what do imbeciles need very, very, very, expensive administration of the law for?

"Natural selection will not remove ignorance from future generations." Dr Richard Dawkins

Adults with the basic skills of a foetus will succeed adults with the basic skills of a child; the former will need only food and shelter.

"We have the power to turn against our creators." Dr Richard Dawkins

ACCURATE SEERS: Then, they foresaw that Britons would be imbeciles (adults with the basic skills of a child), so they embarked on armed robbery and dispossession raids in own AFRICA, and wherever they, and those they armed, used guns to mercilessly slaughter defenceless AFRICANS, they dispossessed them, and whenever they robbed Africans, they took possession, and they used yields of several centuries of merciless RACIST EVIL (the evilest racist terrorism and the greediest economic cannibalism the world will ever know) to create SOCIALIST ELDORADO, and they decommissioned natural selection, and they reversed progressive evolution, and they made it possible for millions of imbeciles to breed more millions of imbeciles.

John, castrate or sterilise imbeciles, including functional semi-illiterate hereditary White Supremacist Freemason Judges.

"An urgent need for depopulation." John Kerry.

The principal beneficiaries of any Antichrist System are the richest in the crooked system.

Joseph, how come Jews are only 1.4% of the population of the USA, and 50% of billionaires in the USA are Jews? "Jews are very good with money." President Trump (45th).

Bianca and Jared Kushner are Jews. Bernard Madoff (1938–2021), Ghislaine Maxwell's dad, Ján Ludvík Hyman

Binyamin Hoch (1923–1991), and Judas Iscariot were Jews.

Facts are sacred.

"The truth allows no choice." Dr Samuel Johnson.

Matthew 2:16: Then, they brainlessly and baselessly self-awarded SUPREME KNOWLEDGE, and they destroyed all those who knew that they were impostors and experts of deception.

Then, they won in crooked courts before crooked Judges, but in the WAR, when the Corporal flipped, the only sinless and transparently just Judge looked away, and very, very, very, greedy bastards, greedier than the grave, and like death, never satisfied—Habakkuk 2:5, lost everything and more—John 5:22, Matthew 25: 31–46.

Then, all Judges were Pure White, and most of them were FREEMASONS, and some of them were THICKER than a gross of planks, and Pure White Freemason Judges who believed that daily dialogues with IMBECILES (adults with the basic skills of a child) was a proper job, which was worthwhile, and manly, were SCAMMERS, and pure White Freemason Judges who demanded and accepted very, very, very, valuable considerations in exchange for daily dialogues with IMBECILES (adults with the basic skills of a child—were THIEVES (racketeers).

"The best opportunity of developing academically and emotional." Bedford's District Judge Paul Robert Ayers, >70, a Mason, and the Senior Vice President of the

Association of Her Majesty's District Judges, 3, St Paul's Square, MK 40 1SQ.

Our opportunist racist pure White bastard was granted the platform to display hereditary prejudice.

Our half-wit is our unashamedly functional semi-illiterate Moron Mason. Perception is grander than reality.

Our MF. Our imbecile Freemason District Judge of our Empire of Stolen Affluence - Habakkuk.

His spinal cord seemed to be his highest centre.

His pure White skin concealed his impure dark black brain. Archie is impure (<100% White).

URANIUM: American and Russian troops are camped side by side in NIGER.

Our own Nigeria: Shell's docile cash cow since 1956. Unlike Putin's Russia, there are no oil wells or gas fields in Freemasons' Luton and where his pure White mother and father of Bedford's District Judge were born. Our own Nigeria babies with huge oil wells and gas fields near their huts eat only 1.5/day in our own NIGERIA, our very, very, very, bellyful pure White bastard, a mere poly-educated former debt-collector Solicitor in NORWICH (5th Rate Partner) whose pure White mother and father have seen CRUDE OIL, and who pure White ancestors, including ultra-righteous pure White John Bunyan (1628 – 1688) were fed like battery hens with yields of stolen children of poor people, including pure Black African ancestors of our impure Black Duchess, Meghan Markle (43% Nigerian), and her impure children (<100% White), was our Senior District Judge in BEDFORD, Great Britain. Which part of our own shithole Africa is great?

An ignorant, ultra-righteous, very, very, very, highly civilised, and super-enlightened descendant of THIEVES and owners of stolen children of poor people, including the pure Black African ancestors of Colin Powell (1937 – 2021).

We are FOREIGNERS in their country, and they have POWER over our life, and they have absolute power over everything that is INFERIOR to our life, our livelihood, and material possessions, but extremely nasty HEREDITARY RACIST BASTARDS do not have any power over our minds while we breathe God's free air.

Percentage of children in the UK hitting educational targets at 5, in descending order:

1. Asian (Indian)

2. Asian (Any other Asian)

3. White (British)

4. White (Irish)

5. Mixed (any other)

6. Mixed (white and black African)

7. Chinese

8. Mixed (White and black Caribbean)

9. Black (African heritage)

10. Asian (Any other Asian)

11. Black (Caribbean heritage)

12. Black (other)

13. Asian (Bangladeshi)

14. White (Any other white)

15. Any other ethnic group

16. Asian (Pakistani)

17. White (Traveller of Irish heritage)

18. White (Gypsy/ Roma).

Source: Centre Forum, 2016.

Children in the UK hitting educational targets at 16, in descending order:

1. Chinese

2. Asian (Indian)

3. Asian (Any other Asian)

4. Mixed (White and Asian)

5. White (Irish)

6. Mixed (Any other)

7. Any other ethnic group

8. Asian (Bangladeshi)

9. Parent/pupil preferred not to say

10. Mixed (White and black African)

11. White (Any other white)

12. Black (African heritage)

13. White (British)

14. Asian (Pakistani)

15. Black (other)

16. Mixed (White and black Caribbean)

17. Black (Caribbean heritage)

18. White (Traveller of Irish heritage)

19. White (Gypsy/ Roma)

Source: Centre Forum, 2016.

Genetic damage is the most enduring residue of European Christians' commerce in millions of stolen African children, including the pure Black African ancestors of our impure Black Duchess, Meghan Markle (43% Nigerian), and her impure children (<100% White).

Slavery irreversibly weakened the common genetic pool of AFRICANS, and irreversible genetic damage is the most enduring residue of European Christians' commerce in millions of stolen children of people, including the pure Black African ancestors of our impure Black Duchess, Meghan Markle (43% Nigerian), and her impure children (<100% White).

If, as it is apparent, Yellow People (Chinese), who were first on the list of those meeting academic targets at age 16, were allowed to choose, they wouldn't allow White Britons whose ethnic group were 13th of the list of those meeting academic targets at age 16—to guide the education of their children. Why should NIGERIANS (Africans), whose ethnic group was above White Britons on the list of those meeting academic targets at age 16, allow a pure White Gypsy-like District Judge, with arbitrarily acquired camouflage English names, and a mere poly-educated former debt-collector Solicitor in NORWICH (5th Rate Partner), whose ethnic (assumed) were last (19th) on the list of those meeting academic targets at 16, have a say in the education of their NIGERIAN children?

Medium

https://medium.com/@yinkabamgbelu45/based-on-available-eviden…

Based on available evidence, Sue Gregory (OBE), Officer of the …

WEBOct 29, 2021 · district judge ayers of bedford county court: a brainless white man; a racist descendant of professional thieves and … Daringtruths—Posts | Facebookwww. facebook.com › Daringtruths01 …

**TWELVE:** Ignorant descendants of THIEVES and owners of stolen children of poor people, including the pure Black African ancestors of our impure Duchess, Meghan Markle (43% Nigerian), and her impure children (<100% White). Members of the brainlessly and baselessly self-awarded SUPERIOR RACE have been lied to at home and at school that the skin colour of foreigners and the accent they employ to speak a foreign language are very, very, very, important parts of intellect.

SLAVERY IS IMMORTAL: Only our visible chains are off, direct descendants of owners of our direct ancestors will never voluntarily remove our true chains. Only excessively stupid Nigg*rs expect others to voluntarily relinquish several centuries-old advantageous positions in exchange for NOTHING. Prior to SLAVERY, apart from the very, very, very, luxuriant land, there was absolutely NOTHING in Great Britain worth stealing. "Agriculture not only gives riches to a nation, but the only one she can call her own." Dr Samuel Johnson. BEDFORD, ENGLAND: District Judge Paul Robert Ayers, >70, a Mason, and the Senior Vice President of the Association of Her Majesty's District Judges, 3, St Paul's Square, MK40 1SQ, our own NIGERIA (oil/gas) is by far more relevant to the economic survival of all your White children than Freemasons' Kempston – Habakkuk.

"Trump's administration packed Courts with White Judges." Kamala Harris

BEDFORD, ENGLAND: District Judge Paul Robert Ayers, > 70, a Mason, and the Senior Vice President of the

Association of Her Majesty's District Judges, 3, St Paul's Square, MK 40 1SQ, the NIGERIAN, from shithole Africa, does not believe in any part of the legal system than you serve, and he has the POWER to use cogent facts and irrefutable evidence to irreversibly destroy you and it.

The pure Black child's sister thanks her stars that the incontrovertibly functional semi-illiterate, closeted racist white man did not have anything to do with her education.

Ignorant ultra-righteous RACIST BASTARDS love brainless and baseless superiority, their self-awarded inviolable birth right, but they don't want Freedom of Expression because they don't want their mentally gentler children and the imbeciles they shepherd to know that only the universally acknowledged irrefutably superior skin colour that they neither made nor chose and God Almighty are truly good (Mark 10:18), and they will be considerably diminished as human beings without it, and they know it.

In her GCSE, the pure Black African child's sister gained the following grades:
English Language A*
English Literature A*
Mathematics A*
Additional Mathematics A*
Physics A*
Chemistry A*
Biology A*
History A*
Latin A

Spanish A
Advanced Level Mathematics A.

Two years later, she gained 6 Advanced Level A Grades.

Age saved the black child from the evil clutches of the closeted racist pure white bastard, a mere Poly-educated former debt-collector Solicitor in Norwich (5th Rate Partner).

OUR OWN NIGERIA: SHELL'S DOCILE CASH COW SINCE 1956: A brainless hereditary RACIST pure White bastard whose pure White mother and father have never seen CRUDE OIL thrives in our own Great Britain. A racist descendant of undocumented refugees from Eastern Europe, with arbitrarily acquired camouflage English names. Based on several decades of very, very, very, proximate observations and direct experiences, they are always looking for new ways to injure our people.

They hate us, more than their ancestors hated ours, and it is plainly deductible that their children will hate ours more than they hate us. Bedford's District Judge Paul Robert Ayers should use his brain to guide the education of his own white children in exactly the same way as his own white father and mother guided him. If he believes that his own white father and mother had very, very strong views about his education, it's proof that he and his white father and mother did not know better.

Poly-educated hereditary racist pure White rubbish. Our unashamedly functional semi-illiterate pure White bastard. Perception is grander than reality. White skin, a huge stolen trust fund, and what else? Before Slavery, what?

The only evidence of his purportedly very, very, very, High IQ, is the stolen affluence that his thoroughly wretched ancestors (mere peasants and agricultural labourers from the mainland Europe) crossed the English Channel, without luggage or decent shoes, to latch onto, and they arbitrarily acquired camouflage English names, and they deceived all their mentally gentler children (OECD) that their ancestors were aboriginal Britons who evolved from black monkeys with tails to tailless white monkeys in the forests of Great Barford, Bedfordshire. There is nothing great in Great Barford, not even one.

A lecherous hereditary racist pure White bastard.

An ignorant ultra-righteous direct descendant of industrial-scale PROFESSIONAL THIEVES and owners of kidnapped children of defenceless Africans ultra-righteously sat on skulls of stolen children of defenceless poor people, more skulls than the millions at the doorstep of Comrade Pol Pot (1925 – 1998) in our Grand Cathedral Court that was preceded by Slavery, future flats.

29, Goldington Road, MK40 3NN, is a block of flats.

"We shall deal with the racist bastards when we get out of prison." Comrade Robert Mugabe (1924 – 2019).

https://youtu.be/rayVcfyu9Tw.

They are more familiar with the descendants of the PLANTATION NEGROES: Descendants of stolen human beings who were unnaturally selected, genetically reversed, artificially bred for labour, and reared like cattle on stolen plantations - Habakkuk.

Then, almost everything was actively and deliberately stolen with guns.

Highly civilised, Christian, and ultra-righteous RACIST ECONOMIC CANNIBALS prayed to God, on their knees, every Sunday, and they persecuted and robbed His Black creations the rest of the week.

The academic height that the pure white father and mother of the closeted racist white District Judge Paul Robert (Bobby) Ayers cannot know, and which the natural talents of all his own white children and grandchildren will not exploit (OECD).

Dr Richard Dawkins and OECD implied that all the White children of Pure White District Judge Paul Robert Ayers, > 70, a Mason, and the Senior Vice President of the Association of Her Majesty's District Judges should be duller than their own verifiably crooked, unashamedly functional semi-illiterate, and opportunist racist pure White bastard father.

"Natural selection will not remove ignorance from future generations." Dr Richard Dawkins

WHITE PRIVILEGE: The public must not know that intellect is absolutely unrelated to the universally acknowledged irrefutably superior skin colour that the very, very, very, fortunate wearer neither made nor chose.

England's young people are near the bottom of the global league table for basic skills. OECD finds 16- to 24-year-olds have literacy and numeracy levels no better than those of their grandparents' generation.

England is the only country in the developed world where the generation approaching retirement is more literate and numerate than the youngest adults, according to the first skills survey by the Organisation for Economic Co-operation and Development.

In a stark assessment of the success and failure of the 720-million-strong adult workforce across the wealthier economies, the economic thinktank warns that in England, adults aged 55 to 65 perform better than 16- to 24-year-olds at foundation levels of literacy and numeracy. The survey did not include people from Scotland or Wales.

The OECD study also finds that a quarter of adults in England have the maths skills of a 10-year-old. About 8.5 million adults, 24.1% of the population, have such basic levels of numeracy that they can manage only one-step tasks in arithmetic, sorting numbers or reading graphs. This is worse than the average in the developed world, where an average of 19% of people were found to have a similarly poor skill base.

ENVY IS A THIEF.

Apart from creating very, very, very, cushy salaried jobs for Solicitors and barristers who FAILED where the public were free to buy services they desired from wherever they wanted, and loads did, and parked their liabilities at the public till where other people spend other people's money on other people, what do imbeciles need very, very, very, expensive administration of English law for?

Adults with the basic skills of a FOETUS will succeed imbeciles (adults with the basic skills of a child), and the former will need food and shelter, not very, very, very, expensive administration of English law.

"Envy is weak." Yul Brynner (1920 - 1985).

Skin colour is a great creation of Almighty God, but it is not the GREATEST.

The brain isn't skin colour; then, we were robbed with guns, in the African bush - Habakkuk.

"Those who have robbed have also lied." Dr Samuel Johnson (1709 - 1784).

Highly civilised and Christian Economic Cannibals who shipped about 200,000 guns annually to West Africa, among those who, then, had no knowledge of treating penetrative gunshot wounds, were neither civilised nor enlightened, and they were certainly not Christian.

TURF WAR: Descendants of robbers want to ban the descendants of the robbed from expressing cogent facts. Ignorant ultra-righteous descendants of THIEVES and owners of stolen children of poor people should fu*k off.

The child sister has since gained a First-Class Science Degree from one of the topmost Universities in the UK. Christ saved her from the evil clutches of the Vulgarly Charitable, Antichrist, and Closeted Racist Freemason Thugs: Mediocre Mafia, New Pharisees, New Good Samaritans (Luke 10: 25 – 37), New Good Shepherd (John 10:11- 18), New God (Freemasons believe that only they and Almighty God are truly good – Mark 10:18; even our own Messiah is not truly good – Psalm 53. Integrity, friendship, respect, and charity: All for one, and one for all. Their people are everywhere, and they control almost everything in Great Britain. They are the Defenders of Faiths, including all the motley assemblies of exotic religions and faiths associated with the 15 Holy Books in the House of Commons, and the Dissenters of THE FAITH – John 14:6.

If members of the vulgarly charitable, Antichrist, and hereditary White Supremacist Freemasonry Quasi-Religion – do not find you very, very, very, THREATENING, it is the conclusive proof that you are ANTICHRIST too. Facebook https://www.facebook.com/Daringtruths01/posts/35813174386594...

Daringtruths - A semi-illiterate former debt-collector... - Facebook

WEB Jan 3, 2022 · District Judge Paul Ayers, Bedford. A fool's approval. Only fools approve mediocrity and immortalise it for eternity! If

District Judge Paul Ayers of Bedford County Court, 3 St Paul's Square. GDC: Richard Hill fabricated reports and ...

**THIRTEEN:** "You will bow. You can't beat the system." Kemi Daramola. I shan't: Exodus 20:5. I know who will: Romans 11, 1 John 4:4. She prays to Christ and pays Antichrist Freemasonry Quasi-Protection-Money (tithe) through the Church of Christ, Brickhill Baptist Church, and Antichrist closeted hereditary White supremacist Freemasons in Kempston answer all her prayers. Vulgarly charitable, Antichrist, and closeted hereditary White Supremacist Freemasonry Quasi-Religion (defenders of faiths are dissenters of the faith—John 14:6) is absolutely incompatible with Christian belief—John 14:6. They want all NIGERIANS, from shithole Africa, to be Born-Again Christians who Freemasons feed through the NHS, and who know only the bible and the NHS, and who believe that FREEMASONS are the New Good Samaritans (Luke 10:25–37), New Good Shepherd (John 10: 11–18), and New God: Deluded and conceited vulgarly charitable, Antichrist, and hereditary White Supremacist bastards believe that only they and Almighty God are truly good—Mark 10:18).

HER MIND SET WAS QUASI-PROSTITUTION.

A woman whose mother was not gainfully employed, and was not economically independent, was more likely to expect to be paid for sex: A QUASI-PROSTITUTE.

She went to university to gain a meal ticket degree, but more to hunt, and to ensnare, fellow university students who could pay her for sex. A glorified prostitute wore Born-Again Christian—as a cloak of deceit.

"A woman is the only hunter who uses herself for bait." Confucius.

Based on several decades of very, very, very, proximate observations and direct experiences, Nigerian women, including Born-Again Christians, want MONEY.

'The great question that has never been answered, and which I have not yet been able to answer, despite my thirty years of research into the feminine soul, is "What does a woman want?" Sigmund Freud (1856 – 1939).

Based on several decades of very, very, very, proximate observations and direct experiences, they are innately extremely wicked people, and they are always looking for new ways to injure NIGERIANS, from shithole Africa, who disagree with members of the baselessly and brainlessly self-awarded SUPERIOR RACE.

Facts are sacred, and they cannot be overstated.

Bedford, England: NHS, GDC, Sue Gregory (OBE), alleged Rotarian (Freemasonry without voodoo and/or occultists' rituals), unrelentingly lied under implied oath— Habakkuk 1:4.

A very, very, very, DISHONEST pure White cougar. A crooked closeted hereditary racist Officer of the Most Excellent Order of our Empire of Stolen Affluence— Habakkuk.

Google: White skin and stolen trust fund. Before Slavery, what?

Bedford's District Judge Ayers: White Skin and Stolen Trust ...Amazon UK.https://www.amazon.co.uk › Bedfords-District-Judge-Ay...Buy Bedford's District Judge Ayers: White Skin and Stolen Trust Fund. Before Slavery, What?: 100% Genetic Nigerian Whistleblowing Mole by Ekweremadu, ... £8.19 · In stock.

"I kept telling you, play the game of chess." Resh Diu.

Since gaining a 5th rate Law Degree at Poly (not Russell Group Second Class Alternative Education-Proverbs 17:16), absolutely nothing about him is based on progressive, colour-blind, and measurable objectivity, not even one—Psalm 53.

He owes almost everything to patronage, Freemasons' patronage.

His nomination and constructive appointment as our Judge by dementing or demented (Alzheimer's disease), hereditary White Supremacist Freemason Lords —was not based on progressive, measurable, and colour-blind objectivity, and it showed.

"The best opportunity of developing academically and emotional." Pure White District Judge Paul Robert (Bobby) Ayers.

Poly-educated brainless hereditary racist pure White bastard. His spinal cord seemed to be his highest centre, and his pure White skin concealed his impure dark black brain.

He approved and immortalised what his poly-educated pure White superiors and supervisors in LUTON authorised. HHJ Perusko studied Law at Poly (not Russell Group Second Class Alternative Education—Proverbs 17:16).

"Someone must be trusted. Let it be the Judges." Lord Denning (1899–1999), a Grandmaster 33rd Degree Freemason (Scottish Rite), and an unapologetic White Supremacist bastard.

Judges are fallible human beings like the rest of us, and no one is good, not even one—Psalm 53, so lots and lots of human beings, including Freemason Judges, are RACISTS.

Only He who has no sin should judge sinners—John 5:22, Matthew 25: 31–46.

"A Saint has a past. A sinner has a future." St Augustine.

Sinners, hereditary racist White Supremacist Freemason Judges should not have the moral credibility to Judge Negro sinners—Matthew 7, John 8:7.

OXFORD, ENGLAND: NHS/GDC, Pure White Mrs Helen Falcon (MBE), Member of GDC Committee (former), a mere dmf, a vulgarly charitable Rotarian (Freemasonry with voodoo and/or occultists' rituals), our Postgraduate Dean, Oxford (former), and the spouse of Pure White Mr Falcon, unrelentingly lied under oath and/or on record—Habakkuk 1:4.

A crooked closeted hereditary racist pure White homunculus cougar. A very, very, very, DISHONEST Member of the Most Excellent Order of our Empire of Stolen Affluence—Habakkuk.

To survive in their RACIST HELL HOLE, we must bow to hereditary racist bastards, ignorant ultra-righteous descendants of THIEVES and owners of stolen children of poor people, including the pure Black African ancestors of our impure Black Duchess, Meghan Markle (43% Nigerian), and her impure children (<100% White), or play hereditary White supremacist bastards like chess.

Facebook

https://www.facebook.com/Daringtruths01/posts/33541181080460...

Daringtruths - GOOGLE: MDDUS HENDERSON LETTERS If Her.

WEBOct 25, 2021 · 15 Aug 2016 - Sir Winston Churchill Based on accessible information, it is the absolute truth that District Judge Ayers of Bedford County Court in . Daringtruths - DISTRICT JUDGE AYERS OF - Facebook https://pt-br.facebook.com › Daringtruths01 › photos › di...

Our poly-educated pure White rubbish was granted the platform to display hereditary prejudice. Only his skin colour is good, and he neither made nor chose it, and he will be considerably diminished as a human being without it, and he knows it.

BEDFORD, ENGLAND: District Judge Paul Robert (Bobby) Ayers, the Nigerian, from shithole Africa, is irreconcilably very, very, very, different from you, and the mind that he did not choose is finer than the system you serve, and he has the POWER to use cogent facts and irrefutable evidence to irreversibly destroy you and it. The fellow is who He says He is—John 14:6. The supernatural exists, and it is always accessible to those who stand where it can come—John 14:26.

"Jesus is the bedrock of my faith." HM (1926–2022).

"They may not have been well written from a grammatical point of view but I am confident I had not forgotten any of the facts." Pure White Geraint Evans, our imbecile England's Class Welsh Postgraduate Tutor, Oxford.

Pure White Mrs Helen Falcon, MBE, Member GDC Committee (former), a mere dmf, a vulgarly charitable Rotarian (Freemasonry without voodoo or occultists' rituals), our Postgraduate Dean, Oxford (former), unrelentingly lied under oath and/or on record—Habakkuk 1:4, and the homunculus crooked cougar, albeit a Member of the Most Excellent Order of our Empire of Stolen Affluence—Habakkuk, nominated, appointed, and instructed Geraint Evans, and those who appointed Mrs Helen Falcon (MBE) paid the salaries of all Judges: Conflict of interest in creeping DPRK.

BEDFORD, ENGLAND: District Judge Paul Robert (Bobby) Ayers, the fellow is He says He is, and He told Jews and others the truth, in the Council, when He disclosed pictures His unbounded mind painted. The mind that the NIGERIAN, from shithole AFRICA, did not choose is finer and clearer than yours, and he has the POWER to use cogent facts and irrefutable evidence to irreversibly destroy you and it.

BEDFORD, ENGLAND: Pure White District Judge Paul Robert (Bobby) Ayers, based on several decades of very, very, very, proximate observations and direct experiences, the legal system you serve is absolutely irreversibly bastardised, indiscreetly DISHONEST, unashamedly mediocre, vindictive, potently weaponised, institutionally RACIST, and overseen by members of the vulgarly charitable, Antichrist, and closeted hereditary White supremacist Quasi-Freemasonry Religion: Mediocre Mafia, New Pharisees, New Good Samaritans (Luke 10:25–37), New Good Shepherd (John 10:11- 18), New God (deluded and conceited Freemasons believe that only they and God Almighty are truly good—Mark 10:18), Defenders of faiths, including the motley assemblies of exotic religions and faiths associated with the 15 Holy Books in the House of Commons, and Dissenters of the faith—John 14:6.

BEDFORD, ENGLAND: Pure White District Judge Paul Robert (Bobby) Ayers, it is plainly deductible that reasoning and vision do not have FINITE BOUNDARIES. The fellow is who He says He is, and when it became apparent to JEWS and GENTILES that the fellow was intellectually unplayable, He was kidnapped and tried in a crooked Court before crooked Judges, and He was killed solely because He spoke, but He was not punished for speaking, but He was killed by intolerant bastards solely to prevent Him from speaking—Matthew 27: 32 -56.

"Freedom of Expression is a basic right." Lady Hale

"I have seen evil, and it has the face of Mark Fuhrman." Johnnie Cochran (1937–2005).

Based on several decades of very, very, very, proximate observations and direct experiences, a White Welsh man is not only a devil, but he is also a THIEF, and he is thoroughly crazy.

WALES, A MERE QUASI-PROVINCE OF ENGLAND: NHS/GDC, Pure White Geraint Evans, England's Class Welsh Postgraduate Tutor, Oxford, England's Class Dentist, Rowtree Dental Care, NN4 0NY, alleged Rotarian (Freemasonry without voodoo and/or occultists' rituals), and the spouse of well-worn and ugly Sue, uglier than the Dalit, Suella Braverman, alias libido killer, unrelentingly lied under implied oath and/or on record—Habakkuk 1:4. A very, very, very, dishonest pure White Welshman. A crooked closeted hereditary racist England's Class Postgraduate Tutor, Oxford.

Medium

https://medium.com/@cole69915/bedford-district-judge-bd94dfc01...

BEDFORD: DISTRICT JUDGE.—Medium

WEBAug 22, 2022 · District Judge Ayers, Bedford. Freemasons teach members secret handshakes, not grammar. GDC: Richard Hill fabricated reports and unrelentingly lied ...

An extremely nasty hereditary White Supremacist bastard was granted the platform to display hereditary prejudice.

"I emphasis the point." Bedford's District Judge Paul Robert (Bobby) Ayers.

He made a mistake, of course he did, and had he not, he would have practised proper Law in Strand instead of daily dialogues with imbeciles in the Lowest Court.

BEDFORD, ENGLAND: District Judge Paul Robert (Bobby) Ayers, based on cogent, irrefutable, and available evidence, the pure White ancestors of your own pure White father and mother were THIEVES and owners of stolen children of poor people, including the pure Black African ancestors of our impure Black Duchess, Meghan Markle (43% Nigerian), and her impure children (<100% White). OUR OWN NIGERIA: SHELL'S DOCILE CASH COW SINCE 1956. Paul, NIGERIA (oil/gas) is by far more relevant to the economic survival of all your White children, your pure White father, your pure White mother, and your pure White spouse than Freemasons' Northampton: OYINBO OMO OLE: THIEVES – HABAKKUK.

FREEMASONS: CULTISTS, RITUALISTS, VOODOO MEN, AND CLOSETED WHITE SUPREMACIST BASTARDS.

Bedfordshire Masonic Centre, the Keep, MK42 8AH. BEDFORD, ENGLAND: NHS/GDC, Freemason, Brother Richard William Hill fabricated reports and unrelentingly lied under oath - Habakkuk 1:4. Facts are sacred, and they cannot be overstated.

URANIUM: Russian and American troops in Niger. Our own Nigerian babies with huge oil wells and gas fields near their huts eat only 1.5/day in our own NIGERIA, a very,

very, very, bellyful unashamed functional semi-illiterate pure White bastard whose pure White father and mother have never seen CRUDE OIL, and whose pure White ancestors, including the pure White ancestors of unapologetic White supremacist 33$^{rd}$ Degree Freemason, Sir Winston Churchill (1874 – 1965), were fed like battery hens with yields of stolen children of defenceless poor people, including the pure Black African ancestors of our impure Black Duchess, Meghan Markle (43% Nigerian), and her impure children (<100% White), was our Senior District Judge in BEDFORD.

RACIST JUDGES: The Quasi-Communist haven for Solicitors and Barristers who FAILED in practice. When Solicitors and Barristers FAILED in practice, loads did, if they were FREEMASONS, they became Judges or something else, if not, they became POLITICIANS or something else.

Based on very, very, very, proximate observations and direct experiences, the pure White man, albeit England's Class Senior Judge, was a RACIST DEVIL. A closeted hereditary racist pure White bastard was granted the platform to display innate RACIAL HATRED—Habakkuk 1:4.

BEDFORD, ENGLAND: NHS/GDC, Sue Gregory (OBE), unrelentingly lied under implied oath—Habakkuk 1:4.

A very, very, very, DISHONEST pure White cougar. A crooked closeted hereditary racist Officer of the Most Excellent Order of our Empire of Stolen Affluence—Habakkuk.

Medium

https://medium.com/@yinkabamgbelu45/bedford-district-judge-our ...

BEDFORD: District Judge, our own Money, NIGERIA (oil/gas) is

WEBNov 3, 2021 · Bedford. District Judge Ayers, 08/06/21. Justice, 08/06/21. Her Honour Judge Gargan. Daringtruths—His Honour Judge Perusko studied at Poly... | Facebook https://en-gb.facebook.com ...

"They may not have been well written from a grammatical point of View." Geraint Evans, England's Class Welsh Imbecile Postgraduate Tutor, Oxford

"The best opportunity of developing academically and emotional." Bedford's District Judge Paul Robert Ayers, >70, a Mason, and the Senior Vice President of the Association of Her Majesty's District Judges, 3, St Paul's Square, MK40 1SQ.

A MORON FREEMASON.

Two, too many, functional semi-illiterate, and pure White hereditary racist bastards were granted the platform, by patronage, to display hereditary prejudice.

Facts are sacred, and they cannot be overstated.

**FOURTEEN:** They are very, very, very, DISHONEST, and they are above all laws, man's, and God's, and they use unbounded and unaccountable powers to guard MERCILESS RACIST EVIL, and they purportedly do everything 'legally': Rules-based procedures, precedent, and statute etcetera. For their legal system to work as designed, they must be SUPERIOR to all foreigners, but they are not, and to balance the unbalanced, crude and cruel hereditary racist bastards resort to EVIL RACIST CRIMINALITY guided and guarded by EVIL RACIST JUDICIAL POWER—Habakkuk 1:4.

GDC Manager: Pure White Jonathan Martin, alleged Rotarian (Antichrist Freemasonry without voodoo or cultists' rituals), unrelentingly lied under implied oath and /or on record—Habakkuk 1:4.

A very, very, very, dishonest pure White man. A mere poly-educated (not Russell Group Second Class Alternative Education—Proverbs 17:16) that parked his liability at the till of dentists' money. A crooked closeted hereditary racist alleged Rotarian (Antichrist Freemasonry without voodoo or cultists' rituals)—Habakkuk 1:4.

"The white man is the devil." Mohammed Ali (1942–2016).

They hate us, and we know. Based on several decades of very, very, very, proximate observations and direct experiences, a White man is not only a devil, but he is also a THIEF, and he is thoroughly crazy.

Our own NIGERIAN BABIES with huge oil wells and gas fields near their huts eat only 1.5/day in our own

NIGERIA, a very, very, very, bellyful Jonathan Martin, Case Work Manager, GDC, a mere poly-educated (not Russell Group Inferior Education—Proverbs 17:16), who parked his liability at the till of dentists' money, and whose pure White mother and father have never seen CRUDE OIL, and whose pure White ancestors, including the pure White ancestors of Aneurin Bevan (1897–1960), were fed like battery hens with yields of stolen children of defenceless poor people, including the pure Black African ancestors of our impure Black Duchess, Meghan Markle (43% Nigerian), and her White children (<100% White), thrives in Great Britain—Habakkuk.

Slavery preceded Aneurin Bevan's NHS, and it paid for it.

GDC: Jonathan Martin's Letters (2010): The Tyranny of ...

Amazon UK

https://www.amazon.co.uk › GDC-Jonathan-Martins-Lett...

GDC: Jonathan Martin's Letters (2010): The Tyranny of the White Majority (GDC—LETTERS Book 1) eBook : Bamgbelu, Yinka: Amazon.co.uk: Kindle Store. £7.74

37, Wimpole Street, London: Jonathan Martin, Case Work Manager, GDC, you are worthy only because you are pure White and England is very, very, very, rich (currently, the six largest economy on earth), apart from those you are PURIFIED NOTHING. It is absolutely impossible for your talent and yields of the land on which your own pure White father and mother were born.

37, Wimpole Street, London: Jonathan Martin, Case Work Manager, GDC: One dimensionally educated pure White rubbish, only the universally acknowledged irrefutably superior skin colour that he neither made nor chose and Almighty God are truly good, and he neither made nor chose it, and he would be considerably diminished as a human being without it, and he knows it.

37, Wimpole Street, London: Jonathan Martin, Case Work Manager, GDC, the mind that the NIGERIAN, from shithole Africa, did not choose, is irreconcilably very, very, very, different from yours, and it is considerably finer than the system you serve, and he has the power to use cogent facts and irrefutable evidence to irreversibly destroy you and it.

37, Wimpole Street, London: Jonathan Martin, Case Work Manager, GDC, pure White man, let me tell you, reasoning and vision do not have finite boundaries, and the supernatural exists, and it is consistently accessible to those who stand where it can come—John 14:26. The fellow is who He says He is.

"Jesus is the bedrock of my faith." HM (1926–2022).

BEDFORD, ENGLAND: District Judge Paul Robert Ayers, >70, a Mason, and Senior Vice President of the Association of Her Majesty's District Judges, 3, St Paul's Square, MK40 1SQ., A brainless hereditary racist pure White bastard, his White children mightn't be able to spell QUADRATIC, and his pure White mother and father mightn't know its meaning.

"I emphasis the point." Bedford's District Judge Paul Robert Ayers, >70, a Mason, and Senior Vice President of the Association of Her Majesty's District Judges, 3, St Paul's Square, MK40 1SQ.

His pure White mother and father mightn't know the meanings of words he couldn't spell, which his mentally gentler White children mightn't be able to read properly.

Perception is grander than reality.

WHITE PRIVILEGE: Everything, absolutely everything is assumed in favour of the universally acknowledged irrefutably superior skin colour that the very, very, very, fortunate wearer neither made nor chose.

A brainless racist pure White bastard, having FAILED in practice, loads did, he parked his liability at the public till, and sold unashamed mediocrity and confusion to the undiscerning

"The best opportunity of developing academically and emotional." Bedford's District Judge Paul Robert Ayers, >70, a Mason, and Senior Vice President of the Association of Her Majesty's District Judges, 3, St Paul's Square, MK40 1SQ.

A MORON FREEMASON.

Facts are sacred, and they cannot be overstated.

His pure White skin concealed his impure dark black brain. An ignorant ultra-righteous descendant of THIEVES and owners of stolen children of poor people, including the pure Black African ancestors of the impure (<100% White) niece and nephew of the Prince of Wales. The last time he passed through the filter of measurable objectivity was when he studied 5th Rate Law at Poly, and absolutely everything else is the GIFT OF PATRONAGE (FREEMASONS), and it showed.

37, Wimpole Street, W1G 8DQ, London: Jonathan Martin, Case Work Manager, GDC, based on cogent, irrefutable, and available evidence, the DNA of GDC is MERCILESS RACIST EVIL guarded but unbounded and unaccountable power, and the control of LOADS of dentists' money, the magnet, and MEAT.

37, Wimpole Street, London: Jonathan Martin, Case Work Manager, GDC, based on cogent, irrefutable, and available evidence, the system you serve is PURIFIED RACIST EVIL, and it is absolutely irreparable.

Antichrist, hereditary racist, and crooked homunculus cougar: Mrs Helen Falcon, MBE, and ROTARIAN (Freemasonry without voodoo and/or occultists' rituals), was incompetently DISHONEST, mediocre, and indiscreetly RACIST. The pure White ancestors of her pure White father and mother were incompetent RACIST LIARS too, they were THIEVES and owners and stolen children of poor people, including the pure Black African ancestors of our impure Black Duchess, Meghan Markle (43% Nigerian), and her impure children (<100% White).

How could we be so stupid not to realise that these characters are genetic RACIST BASTARDS, and we voluntarily brought children to their RACIST HELL

HOLE, and will leave them there? We are stupider than morons who made WHITE MASTERS richer by voluntarily making SLAVE BABIES on plantations.

Mrs Helen Falcon, MBE, crooked, hereditary racist, and vulgarly charitable Antichrist Rotarian.

If Antichrist ROTARIANS (Freemasonry without voodoo and/or occultists' rituals) do not find you threatening, it is the conclusive proof that you are Antichrist too.

OXFORD, ENGLAND: On November 25, 2009, based on very, very, very, proximate observations, and direct experiences, Mrs Helen Falcon (MBE) exuded EVIL ENERGY, and there was something of the midnight about the homunculus, crooked, and closeted hereditary RACIST pure cougar (Anne Widdecombe).

OXFORD, ENGLAND: NHS, GDC, Mrs Helen Falcon (MBE), Member of GDC Committee (former), a mere dmf, a Rotarian (Freemasonry without voodoo and/or occultists' rituals), our Postgraduate Dean, Oxford (former), and the spouse of Mr Falcon, unrelentingly lied under oath and/or on record—Habakkuk 1:4.

A very, very, very, dishonest pure White woman.

A crooked closeted hereditary racist Rotarian (Freemasonry without voodoo and/or occultists' rituals), expectedly was not deterred by His Justice (John 5:22, Matthew 25:31-46) because the homunculus crooked racist cougar did not believe in His exceptionalism— John 14:6.

How could we be so stupid not to realise that these characters are genetic RACIST BASTARDS, and we voluntarily brought children to their RACIST HELL HOLE, and will leave them here? We are stupider than morons who made WHITE MASTERS richer by voluntarily making SLAVE BABIES on cotton and cane plantations.

John 14:26: If a SUPERNATURAL POWER comes only to those who stand where it can come, and if the only way of knowing that you are standing where it can come is because it came to you, and if those it did not come to believe that those it came to are LUNATICS, it is because those who believe that what they cannot see does not exist are excessively stupid. Insanity may respond to pills, excessive stupidity has no cure.

"There is no sin except stupidity." Wilde

Mrs Helen Falcon (MBE), Member of GDC Committee (former), a mere dmf, a Rotarian (Freemasonry without voodoo and/or occultists' rituals), our Postgraduate Dean, Oxford (former), and the spouse of Mr Falcon, the NIGERIAN, from shithole Africa, does not believe in any part of the system you served, as no part of it is good, no even one—Psalm 53, and the mind that he did not choose is finer than it, and he has the power to use cogent facts and irrefutable evidence to irreversibly destroy you and it. You are worthy only because you are pure White and England is very, very, very rich (currently, the six largest economy in the world), apart from those, you are PURIFIED NOTHING. Unlike Putin's Russia, there are no oil wells or gas fields in Corby (Little Glasgow) and where your own pure White mother and father were born. It is absolutely impossible for your talent and yields of the land on which your own pure White father and mother were born to sustain your very, very, very, high standard of living. The pure White ancestors of your own pure White father and mother were THIEVES and owners of stolen children of defenceless poor people, including the pure Black African of our impure Black Duchess, Meghan Markle (43% Nigerian), and her impure children (<100% White).

"The white man is the devil." Elijah Mohammed (1897–1975).

Facts are sacred, and they cannot be overstated.

Based on several decades of very, very, very, proximate observations and direct experiences, a White woman is not only a DEVIL (Jezebel), but she is also a THIEF, and she is crazy—Habakkuk 1:4.

OXFORD, ENGLAND: GDC/NHS/MPS/BDA, British Soldier, Territorial Defence, Stephanie Twidale (TD), unrelentingly lied under oath—Habakkuk 1:4. A very, very, very, dishonest pure White cougar. A closeted hereditary racist BRITISH SOLDIER (TD).

The YANKS are NATO, and absolutely everything is an auxiliary bluff.

Facebook

https://www.facebook.com/daringtruths01/posts/racist-bastards-w...

Daringtruths—Racist bastards want skin colour…—Facebook

WEBNov 11, 2021 · DISTRICT JUDGE AYERS,which part of BEDFORD COUNTY COURT is the yield of TRANSPARENT VIRTUE: The building or its chattels? An IGNORANT FOOL;a RACIST descendant of THIEVES and owners of STOLEN HUMAN BEINGS BEDFORD:Dr Richard Hill fabricated reports and LIED under oath. HABAKKUK The best opportunity of developing …

**FIFTEEN:** The administration of their law is a NEGROPHOBIC CHARADE that is overseen by CLOSETED WHITE SUPREMACIST FREEMASONS. Incompetent art incompetently imitates life.

GDC: 37, Wimpole Street, W1G 8DQ, based on cogent, irrefutable, and available evidence, Geraint Evans, Dentist, Rowtree Dental Care, NN4 0NY, unrelentingly LIED under implied oath and/or on record—Habakkuk 1:4.

A crooked, hereditary racist, and very, very, very, dishonest, pure White Welshman.

He was not deterred by His Justice (John 5:22) because he did not believe in His exceptionalism—John 14:6.

Based on several decades of very, very, very, proximate observations and direct experiences, the potent weapon of the hereditary racist privileged dullard the direct descendant of the father of lies (John 8:44, John 10:10) is the mother of RACIST LIES, and her power is the certainty that all Judges will be White, and her hope is that all Judges would be RACIST BASTARDS too.

His type KILLED the Indian dentist, only 42, albeit hands-off, with the mens rea hidden in the belly of the actus reus.

Google: Dr Anand Kamath, dentist.

BEDFORD, ENGLAND: District Judge Paul Robert Ayers, >70, a Mason, and Senior Vice President of the Association of Her Majesty's District Judges, 3, St Paul's Square, MK40 1SQ, apart from debt-collection, what was in Norwich for functional semi-illiterate Freemason Solicitors to do?

BEDFORD, ENGLAND: District Judge Paul Robert Ayers, >70, a Mason, and Senior Vice President of the Association of Her Majesty's District Judges, 3, St Paul's Square, MK40 1SQ, it is not the truth that daily dialogues with IMBECILES, including pure White Welsh imbecile, England's Class Postgraduate Tutor, Oxford, is a proper job that is worthwhile and manly.

"They may not have been well written from a grammatical point of view but I am confident I had not forgotten any of the facts." Geraint Evans, England's Class Welsh Postgraduate Tutor, Oxford.

AN IMBECILE: AN ADULT WITH THE BASIC SKILLS OF A CHILD.

Our own NIGERIAN BABIES with huge oil wells and gas fields near their huts eat only 1.5/day in our own NIGERIA, a very, very, very, bellyful pure White Welsh imbecile whose pure White Welsh mother and father have never seen CRUDE OIL, and whose pure White Welsh ancestors, including the pure White Welsh ancestors of Aneurin Bevan (1897–1960), were fed like battery hens with yields of stolen children of poor people, including the pure Black African ancestors of the impure (<100% White) niece and nephew of the Prince of Wales, was our Postgraduate Tutor, Oxford.

Aneurin Bevan's NHS was preceded by SLAVERY and paid for it.
Facts are sacred, and they cannot be overstated.
Then, in the Valleys, including in Nick Griffin's Llanerfyl Powys, there were scores of thousands of white sheep and

people, and all the white sheep but not all the people were incestuously conceived, and all the white sheep but not all the people were excessively stupid.

"There is no sin except stupidity." Wilde.

Our closeted hereditary racist and unashamedly functional semi-illiterate pure White impartial Judge – Habakkuk 1:4.

Matthew 14: John was jailed only because he spoke, and the intolerant lunatic Jew removed his head solely to permanently prevent him from speaking.

BEDFORD, ENGLAND: District Judge Paul Robert Ayers, >70, a Mason, and Senior Vice President of the Association of Her Majesty's District Judges, 3, St Paul's Square, MK40 1SQ, our own MONEY, Nigeria (oil/gas) is by far more relevant to the economic survival of all your own White children, your pure White spouse, your pure White mother, and your pure White father than Freemasons' Northampton.

BEDFORD, ENGLAND: District Judge Paul Robert Ayers, >70, a Mason, and Senior Vice President of the Association of Her Majesty's District Judges, 3, St Paul's Square, MK40 1SQ, you are not a SAINT. The pure White ancestors of your own pure White father and mother were THIEVES: Extremely nasty RACIST MURDERERS, nastier than Yevgeny Prigozhin (1961–2023), industrial-scale armed robbers, armed land grabbers, gun runners, drug dealers (opium merchants), and owners of stolen children of poor people, including the pure Black ancestors of our impure Black Duchess, Meghan Markle (43% Nigerian), and her impure children (<100%).

Facts are sacred, and they cannot be overstated.

"The truth allows no choice." Dr Samuel Johnson

The pattern of merciless RACIST EVIL is the same everywhere in their country.

Abuse of temporary power is the fullest definition of RACIST EVIL.

"Those who have the power to do wrong with impunity seldom wait long for the will." Dr Samuel Johnson
BEDFORD, ENGLAND: GDC/NHS, Sue Gregory (OBE), alleged Rotarian (Freemasonry without occultists' rituals and/or voodoo), unrelentingly lied under implied oath—Habakkuk 1:4.

 A very, very, very, dishonest pure White cougar. A crooked closeted hereditary racist Officer of the Most Excellent Order of our Empire of STOLEN AFFLUENCE—Habakkuk.

Based on several decades of very, very, very, proximate observations and direct experiences, theirs is irreparably bastardised, indiscreetly dishonest, unashamedly mediocre, vindictive, potently weaponised, and overseen by members of the vulgarly charitable, hereditary White supremacist, and Antichrist Freemasonry Quasi-Religion: Mediocre Mafia, New Pharisees, New Good Samaritans (Luke 10:25–37), New Good Shepherd (John 10: 11–18), New God (deluded and conceited hereditary racist bastards believe that only they and God Almighty are truly good—Mark 10:18; integrity, friendship, respect, and charity: All for one, and one for all), Defenders of Faiths, including the motley assemblies of exotic FAITHS and RELIGIONS associated with the 15 Holy Books in the House of Commons, and Dissenters of THE FAITH (John 14:6).

They hate us, and we know.

Medium

https://medium.com/@cole69915/closeted-racist-descendants-of-ul…

CLOSETED RACIST DESCENDANTS OF ULTRA-RIGHTEOUS WHITE THIEVES. BEDFORD …

WEBAug 17, 2022 · District Judge Ayers, Bedford. Freemasons teach members secret handshakes, not grammar. GDC: Richard Hill fabricated reports and unrelentingly lied under oath. GDC: Kevin Atkinson (NHS …

Unlike Putin's Russia, there are no oil wells or gas fields in MASONS' KEMPSTON and where the pure White mum and dad of Bedford's Judge were born. He is a functional semi-illiterate. He is rich, and he DISHONESTLY implied that he did not know that his ancestors were THIEVES and owners of stolen children of poor people, including the pure Black African ancestors of our impure Black Duchess, Meghan Markle 43% Nigerian), and her impure children (<100% White) – Habakkuk. Facts are sacred, and they cannot be overstated.

BEDFORD, ENGLAND: Pure White District Judge Paul Robert Ayers, >70, a Mason, and the Senior Vice President of the Association of Her Majesty's District Judges, 3, St

Paul's Square, MK40 ISQ, you are not a SAINT. You are a LEECH, and for several continuous centuries, the pure White ancestors of your own pure White mother and father were extremely nasty, and merciless, RACIST MURDERERS, nastier than Yevgeny Prigozhin (1961–2023), industrial-scale professional THIEVES, and ultra-righteous, very, very, very, highly civilised, and super-enlightened owners of stolen children of poor people, including the pure Black African ancestors of Kamala Harris.

Kamala Harris did not say that Trump's administration packed courts with Mediocre Pure White Judges.

"The truth allows no choice." Dr Samuel Johnson.

"Affluence is not a birth right." Lord Cameron.

Perception is grander than reality.

WHITE PRIVILEGE: Everything, absolutely everything, is assumed in favour of the universally acknowledged irrefutably SUPERIOR SKIN COLOUR that the very, very, very, fortunate wearer neither made nor chose.

Universally acknowledged irrefutably superior skin colour, a huge stolen trust fund, and what else?

Before Slavery what?

OYINBO OMO OLE: THIEVES—HABAKKUK.

They hate us, and we know. Since their ancestors found ours in the African bush in the 15th Century, things have turned out very, very, very, bad for Africa and Africans. Then, greedy racist bastards carried and sold millions of our own Africa's children. Now THIEVES steal our own Africa's natural resources.

SUBSTITUTION IS FRAUDULENT EMANCIPATION.

"Moderation is a virtue only among those who are thought to have found alternatives." Henry Kissinger (1923–2023).

Facts are sacred, and they cannot be overstated.

Based on several decades of very, very, very, proximate observations and direct experiences, the only BLACK racist bastards truly love is MONEY, and absolutely everything else is DECEIT.

BEDFORD, ENGLAND: District Judge Paul Robert Ayers, >70, a Mason, and the Senior Vice President of the Association of Her Majesty's District Judges, 3, St Paul's Square, MK40 ISQ, our own money, NIGERIA (oil/gas) is by far more relevant to the economic survival of all your own White children, your pure White mother, your pure White father, and your pure White spouse than Freemasons' Kempston.

You are PURIFIED FROTH.

You are worthy only because you are pure White and England is very, very, very, rich (currently, the sixth largest economy in the world), apart from those, you are PURIFIED NOTHING.

Based on very, very, very, proximate observations and direct experiences, it is absolutely impossible for your Christ-granted talents and yields of the land on which your own pure White mother and father were norm to sustain your very, very, very, high standard of living.

The pure White ancestors of your own pure White father and mother were THIEVES.

Google: Habakkuk.

An ignorant ultra-righteous descendant of THIEVES and owners of stolen children of poor people, including the pure Black African ancestors Colin Powell (1937–2021).

OYINBO OMOLE: THIEVES—HABAKKUK.

Google: Antichrist Western Civilization: The End Game.

Amazon.com.au

https://www.amazon.com.au/Antichrist-Western-Civilization-Ancestors...

Antichrist Western Civilization: The End Game: Sir, Mr. Justice ...

WebAntichrist Western Civilization: The End Game: Sir, Mr. Justice Haddon Cave KC: Your Ancestors were Thieves and Owners of Stolen Children of Poor Africans ... (England: A ...

Author: Ngozi Ekweremadu

"Sometimes people don't want to hear the truth because they don't want their illusions destroyed." Friedrich Nietzsche (1844–1900).

**SIXTEEN:** BEDFORD, ENGLAND: Pure White District Judge Paul Robert Ayers, >70, a Mason, and the Senior Vice President of the Association of Her Majesty's District Judges, 3, St Paul's Square, MK40 ISQ, the Nigerian, from shithole Africa, does not believe in any part of the legal system you served, as no part of it is good, not even one— Psalm 53. The mind that the NIGERIAN, from shithole Africa, did not choose is finer than the legal system you served, and he has the POWER to use cogent facts and irrefutable evidence to irreversibly destroy you and it. A grossly overrated pure White rubbish: Perception is grander than reality.

BEDFORD, ENGLAND: Pure White District Judge Paul Robert Ayers, >70, a Mason, and the Senior Vice President of the Association of Her Majesty's District Judges, 3, St Paul's Square, MK40 ISQ, the supernatural exists, and it is consistently accessible to those who stand where it can come—John 14:26. Pure White man, let me tell you, you are free to believe or disbelieve, but usurping power, and using stolen power (unelected) to stifle the basic right to disclose pictures painted by free minds—is criminalised cowardice.

The colour bar was crude and cruel. The reasoning bar is spineless cowardice.

"Freedom of Expression is a basic right." Lady Hale

"Find the truth and tell it." Harold Pinter (1930–2008).

BEDFORD, ENGLAND: Pure White District Judge Paul Robert Ayers, >70, a Mason, and the Senior Vice President of the Association of Her Majesty's District Judges, 3, St

Paul's Square, MK40 1SQ, based on several decades of very, very, very, proximate observations and direct experiences, you are relevant only because you are pure White and England is very, very, very, rich (currently, the sixth largest economy on earth), what else? Before slavery, what? Then, there was only subsistence feudal agriculture.

"Agriculture not only gives riches to a nation, but the only one she can call her own." Dr Samuel Johnson

Matthew 19:21: Joseph, how come Jews make up only 1.4% of the population of America, and 50% of the Billionaires in America are Jews?

BEDFORD, ENGLAND: NHS/GDC, Sue Gregory (OBE), unrelentingly lied under implied oath. A very, very, very, dishonest, crooked, and hereditary racist Officer of the Most Excellent Order of our Empire of Stolen Affluence—Habakkuk.

BEDFORD, ENGLAND: Pure White District Judge, the fellow is who He says He is—John 14:6.

"Jesus is the bedrock of my faith." HM (1926–2022).

Then, when they FU*KED, which was very, very, very, often, GENIUS JEWS were their go-to-people, and they would bury RACIST EVIL, and if they couldn't, they would bury the witness and/or victim, and tie all loose ends by every means necessary.

"Jews are intelligent and creative, Chinese are intelligent but not creative, Indians are servile, and Africans are MORONS." Professor James Watson (DNA) paraphrased.

"The white man was created a devil, to bring chaos upon the earth." Malcom X (1925–1965)

Then, all Judges were pure White, and most of them were FREEMASONS, and some of them were THICKER than a gross of planks.

Based on several decades of very, very, very, proximate observations and direct experiences, a White woman is not only a devil, but she is also a THIEF, and she is thoroughly crazy.

BEDFORD, ENGLAND: Pure White District Judge, which part of our Bedfordshire Masonic Centre did the pure White ancestors of your own pure White mother and father buy, or which part of the Grand Cathedral-Building, the Keep, MK42 8AH, preceded SLAVERY: The building or its chattels?

Ignorance is bliss.

"Those who know the least obey the best." George Farquhar (1677–1707).

New Herod (Matthew 2:16, Matthew 14): Ignorant, ultra-righteous, and very, very, very, shallow hereditary racist pure White bastards (predominantly but not exclusively pure White) see molecules and they mercilessly destroy all NIGERIANS, from shithole Africa, who see quarks.

Ignorant racist bastards, and ultra-righteous descendants of THIEVES, owners of stolen children of poor people, and CHRIST KILLERS: The Romans were here for several centuries from 55BC. When it became apparent to them that the fellow was intellectually unplayable, they killed

Him. Our own Messiah was not punished for speaking, but He was killed by intolerant bastards solely to prevent Him from speaking—Matthew 27: 32 -56.

THE LUNATIC NEGRO CARD: Any Nigerian, from shithole Africa, who disagrees with members of the brainlessly and baselessly self-awarded SUPERIOR RACE, is a LUNATIC.

Rather than lose an open debate against a mere NIGG*R, hereditary White supremacist bastards bring out their THUNDER, the Lunatic Negro Card

BEDFORD, ENGLAND: Pure White District Judge Paul Robert Ayers, >70, a Mason, and Senior Vice President of the Association of Her Majesty's District Judges, 3, St Paul's Square, MK40 1SQ, our own money, NIGERIA (oil/gas) is by far more relevant to the economic survival of all your White children than LUTON.

"They may not have been well written from a grammatical point of view." Geraint Evans, Postgraduate Tutor, Oxford

Rishi Sunak, how does our world benefit from using Nuclear Bombs to guard the continuing propagation of IMBECILES?

Facebook

https://www.facebook.com/daringtruths01/posts/racist-bastards-w...

Daringtruths—Racist bastards want skin colour...—Facebook

WEBNov 11, 2021 · DISTRICT JUDGE AYERS,which part of BEDFORD COUNTY COURT is the yield of TRANSPARENT VIRTUE: The building or its chattels? An IGNORANT FOOL;a RACIST descendant of THIEVES and owners of STOLEN HUMAN BEINGS BEDFORD:Dr Richard Hill fabricated reports and LIED under oath. HABAKKUK The best opportunity of developing …

BEDFORD, ENGLAND: District Judge Paul Robert Ayers, >70, a Mason, and Senior Vice President of the Association of Her Majesty's District Judges, 3, St Paul's Square, MK40 1SQ, apart from debt-collection, what was in NORWICH for the brainless pure White bastard to do? He was our District Judge in BEDFORD because he fu*king couldn't do anything else. A very, very, very, hardened racist pure White bastard was granted the platform to display hereditary prejudice.

1976 – 2022: Having FAILED in practice, loads did, the unashamedly functional semi-illiterate pure White bastard parked his liability at the public till and sold unashamed mediocrity and confusion to the undiscerning in exchange for very, very, very, valuable consideration: QUASI-COMMUNISM.

The pure White Senior District Judge and the imbeciles who sat before him were intellectually worthless.

Oyinbo okeleru, osu le meji gbogbo salanga kun.

WHITE PRIVILEGE: If one's skin colour is universally acknowledged to be irrefutably superior, but if one's intellect is not, it is plainly deductible that Freedom of Expression is not one's friend.

Google: Bedford's District Judge Ayers, a Racist Mason.

https://www.youtube.com/watch?v=BlpH4hG7m1A.

"A complaints such as Mrs Bishop's could trigger an enquiry." Stephen Henderson, dentist, LLM, BDS, alleged Rotarian (Freemasonry without voodoo and/or occultists' rituals), and Head at MDDUS, 1 Pemberton Row, London EC4A 3BG.

A brainless, crooked, and hereditary racist pure White bastard immortalised in writing what his supervisors authorised.

Having FAILED in practice, loads did, the hereditary racist pure White bastard parked his liability at the till of dentists' money.

"Yes, Sir, it does her honour, but it would do nobody else honour. I have, indeed, not read it all. But when I take up the end of a web and find a packthread, I do not expect to find embroidery." Dr Samuel Johnson.

'He who couldn't, and FAILED in practice, protected those who could, and PASSED.' George Bernard Shaw paraphrased.

"This and no other is the root from which a tyrant springs, when he first appears he is a protector." Plato.

It is plainly deductible that since 1984, apart from the froth the brainless, crooked, and hereditary racist pure White bastard bought in Cardiff, in 2005, the only examination he did not FAIL is the one he did not do.

Perception is grander than reality, everything, absolutely everything, is baselessly and brainlessly assumed in favour of the universally acknowledged irrefutably superior skin colour that the very, very, very, fortunate wearer neither made nor chose.

WHITE PRIVILEGE: They are not the only creation of Almighty God, and they are not immortal, and the universally acknowledged irrefutably superior skin colour that the very, very, very, fortunate wearer neither made nor chose is not the only wonder of our world, and she would be considerably diminished as a human being without it, and she knows it.

NORTHAMPTONSHIRE, ENGLAND: NHS/GDC, Ms Rachael Bishop, Senior NHS Nurse unrelentingly lied under oath—Habakkuk 1:4.

A very, very, very, dishonest pure White cougar. A crooked closeted hereditary racist Senior NHS Nurse.

They were all pure White: Archie is impure (<100% White).

Based on several decades of very, very, very, proximate observations and direct experiences, homogeneity in the administration of their law is the impregnable secure mask of merciless RACIST EVIL.

They hate us, and we know. Their hairs stand on end when they are challenged by mere NIGERIANS, from shithole

Africa; we and our type are the ones racist bastards will beat up without the support of the YANKS.

If Freemasons have voodoo, and if their occultists' rituals give them access to the supernatural, the vulgarly charitable, Antichrist, and hereditary White supremacist bastards should, directly, use extreme violence to evict PUTIN from Avdiivka, he used extreme violence to convert it from bricks to rubble, and stole it.

"The white man is the devil." Mohammed Ali (1942–2016).

Based on several decades of very, very, very, proximate observations and direct experiences, a White British Soldier, our Territorial Defender (TD) was not only a devil (Jezebel), but she was also a THIEF, and she was thoroughly crazy.

OXFORD, ENGLAND: NHS/GDC/MPS/BDA, British Soldier, Stephanie Twidale (TD), and alleged Rotarian (Freemasonry without voodoo and/or occultists' rituals), unrelentingly lied under oath—Habakkuk 1:4.

A very, very, very, dishonest pure White cougar, albeit a British Soldier (Territorial Defence). A crooked closeted hereditary racist alleged Rotarian (Freemasonry without voodoo and/or occultists' rituals).

The YANKS are NATO, and absolutely everything else is an auxiliary bluff.

President Joseph Biden and President Zelensky want all Ukrainians to be part of our very, very, very, highly civilised, and super-enlightened free world, pure White people, only pure White people, are allowed to fabricate reports and tell incompetent RACIST LIES under oath, but President Putin doesn't, so he used extreme violence to convert Bakhmut from bricks to rubble and stole it.

BEDFORD, ENGLAND: District Judge Paul Robert Ayers, pure White man, let me tell you, the mind that the NIGERIAN, from shithole Africa, did not choose, is finer than the legal system you served, and he does not believe in any part of it, and he has the POWER to use cogent facts and irrefutable evidence to irreversibly destroy you and it.

BEDFORD, ENGLAND: District Judge Paul Robert Ayers, >70, a Mason, and Senior Vice President of the Association of Her Majesty's District Judges, 3, St Paul's Square, MK40 1SQ, pure White man, let me tell you, reasoning and vision do not have finite boundaries. The fellow is who He says He is—John 14:6, and He told Jews and Gentiles the truth when He disclosed pictures His unbounded mind painted.

Based on cogent, irrefutable, and available evidence, the supernatural exists, and it is consistently accessible to those who stand where it can come—John 14:26.

"Jesus is the bedrock of my faith." HM (1926–2022).

The worst they can do to us is to kill us, and they must die too, as the endless state of non-being is our common destiny—Ecclesiastes. We shall go, and they must come—2 Samuel 12:23.

Based on several decades of very, very, very, proximate observations and direct experiences, they are innately extremely wicked people. They hate us, and we know, and they are always looking for new ways to injure us—'LEGALLY'.

"The white man is the devil." Elijah Mohammed (1897–1975).

Based on cogent, irrefutable, and available evidence, a White woman is not only a DEVIL (Jezebel), but she is also a THIEF, and she is thoroughly crazy. Facts are sacred, and they cannot be overstated.

A brainless hereditary racist crooked pure White bastard sat on a highchair that the imbeciles who sat before her couldn't and didn't buy, in our own GRAND CATHEDRAL COURT that was preceded by SLAVERY, future flats.

29, Goldington Road, MK40 3NN, is a block of flats.

BEDFORD, ENGLAND: NHS/GDC, Sue Gregory (OBE), alleged Rotarian (Freemasonry without voodoo and/or occultists' rituals), unrelentingly lied under implied oath—Habakkuk 1:4.

A very, very, very, dishonest pure White cougar. A crooked closeted hereditary racist Officer of the Most Excellent Order of our Empire of Stolen Affluence—Habakkuk.

Her type KILLED the Nigerian GP, Richard Bamgboye, only 56, and the Indian Dentist, Anand Kamath, only 42. Like Alexei Navalny, only 47, Anand and Richard did not die naturally, they were KILLED, albeit hands-off, with the mens rea hidden in the belly of the actus reus.

Facts are sacred, and they cannot be overstated.

**SEVENTEEN:** "Jews are intelligent and creative, Chinese are intelligent but not creative, Indians are servile, and AFRICANS are morons." Professor James Watson (DNA) paraphrased.

Then, when they fu*ked, which was very, very, very, often, Genius Jews were their go-to-people, and if Genius Jews couldn't bury HEREDITARY RACIAL HATRED, they tied all loose ends possible, by burying the victim and/or witness of HEREDITARY MERCILESS RACIST EVIL.

They are not deterred by His Justice (John 5:22, Matthew 25:31–46), because they do not believe in His exceptionalism—John 14:6.

They have only one method of destroying NIGERIANS, from shithole Africa, who disagree with members of the baselessly and brainlessly self-awarded superior race: They start by criminally attaching MERCILESS RACIST EVIL to our people, and they do RACIAL HATRED until it takes hold, and when it does, they instantly revert to LEGALITY, the legality whose entire foundation is HEREDITARY RACIAL HATRED and FRAUD.

Based on several decades of very, very, very, proximate observations and direct experiences, they are PURIFIED EVIL – Habakkuk 1:4.

If members of the vulgarly charitable, Antichrist, and closeted hereditary White supremacist Freemasonry Quasi-Religion do not see you as a threat, it is the conclusive proof that you are Antichrist too.

Based on several decades of very, very, very, proximate observations and direct experiences, their people are everywhere, absolutely everywhere, in their country, and they control almost everything, including RACIAL HATRED and FRAUD. Integrity, friendship, respect, and charity: All for one, and one for all—Habakkuk 1:4.

They are a properly organised gang of extremely nasty hereditary racist bastards who wear vulgar Pharisees' charitable works as cloaks of DECEIT, and use very, very, very, expensive colourful aprons, with vulgar embroideries, to decorate the temples of their powerless and useless fertility tools, and they lie that they don't lie—Psalm 144.

"Lies are told all the time." Sir Michael Havers (1923 - 1992).

They steal POWER, and they use stolen power to prosecute a latent but very, very, very, potent RACE WAR.

They brainlessly and baselessly awarded themselves SUPREME KNOWLEDGE, and they vindictively, and criminally, annul the formal education of Nigerians, from shithole Africa, who disagree with members of the brainlessly and baselessly self-awarded SUPERIOR RACE, and they maliciously persecute our people for the dark coat that we neither made nor chose, and cannot change, and they criminally steal yields of our people's Christ-granted talents, and they impede the ascent of our people from the bottomless crater into which their very, very, very, greedy racist bastard ancestors threw ours, in the African bush, unprovoked, during several continuous centuries of MERCILESS RACIST EVIL: The evilest racist terrorism and the greediest economic cannibalism the world will ever know. Based on several decades of very, very, very, proximate observations and direct experiences, they ARE greedier than the grave, and like death, they are never satisfied—Habakkuk 2:5. They criminally economically strangulate NIGERIANS, from shithole Africa, who disagree with members of the brainlessly and baselessly self-awarded SUPERIOR RACE, and they maliciously place insurmountable obstacles before our people, and they sadistically irreversibly damage the minds of our people, and they mercilessly KILL our own people, albeit hands-off.

Google: Dr Richard Bamgboye, GP.

Google: Dr Anand Kamath, Dentist.

They hate us, and we know. When HERDITARY RACIAL HATRED unravels, ignorant ultra-righteous descendants of THIEVES and owners of stolen children of poor people, including the pure Black African ancestors of our impure Black Duchess, Meghan Markle (43% Nigerian), and her impure children (<100% White), bring out the LUNATIC NEGRO CARD.

Any NIGERIAN, from shithole Africa, who disagrees with members of the brainlessly and baselessly self-awarded superior race is INSANE.

Ignorant, foolish, and hereditary racist bastards see molecules, and they' KILL' all Nigerians, from shithole Africa, who see quarks.

"To disagree with three—fourths of the British public on all points is one of the first elements of sanity, one of the deepest consolations in all moments of spiritual doubt." Wilde

**EIGHTEEN:** When it became apparent that our own MESSIAH was intellectually unplayable, He was KILLED only because He spoke, and He was not punished for speaking, OUR OWN MESSIAH was murdered solely to prevent Him from speaking—Matthew 27:32 -56.

"Sorry, I am a free speech absolutist." Elon Musk.

Then, very, very, very, greedy bastards won in crooked courts before crooked Judges, but in WAR, when the Corporal flipped, the real Judge looked away, and very, very, very, greedy bastards lost everything, and lots and lots more—John 5:22, Matthew 25: 31–46.

LATENT BUT VERY POTENT TURF WAR: Descendants of aliens with arbitrarily acquired camouflage English names, oppress NIGERIAN (and others) descendants of the robbed, with yields of the robbery.

BEDFORD, ENGLAND: Pure White District Judge Paul Robert Ayers, >70, a Mason, and Senior Vice President of the Association of Her Majesty's District Judges, 3, St Paul's Square, MK40 1SQ, what is your pure White father's real name, where did he come from, and when? Or did the pure White ancestors of your own pure White father and mother evolve from black monkeys with tails to tailless white monkeys—in the forests of Freemasons' LUTON?

Ignorance is bliss.

"There is no sin except stupidity." Wilde.

Mustafa Mehmet is Turkish, but Boris Johnson is not. Ali Kemal (1869–1922) crossed the English Channel, in 1909, and without luggage or decent shoes.

The real name of Ghislaine Maxwell's dad was Ján Ludvík Hyman Binyamin Hoch, and he came from Czechoslovakia, with NOTHING, in the 1940s.

Gigantic yields of millions of stolen children of poor people, including the pure Black African ancestors of our impure Black Duchess, Meghan Markle (43% Nigerian), and her impure children (<100 White), not feudal agriculture, lured the Jewish ancestors of Benjamin Disraeli (1804–1881) to Great Britain. Then, Jews followed the money, stolen money—Habakkuk.

Before Slavery, what?

Then, there was only subsistence feudal agriculture.

"Agriculture not only gives riches to a nation, but the only one she can call her own." Dr Samuel Johnson.

URANIUM WAR: American and Russian soldiers are in Niger. Then, very, very, very, greedy racist bastards carried and sold stolen children of poor people, now THIEVES steal our own Africa's natural resources. "How Europe underdeveloped Africa." Dr Walter Rodney (1942–1980).

It is deceit that substitution is EMANCIPATION.

"Moderation is a virtue only among those who are thought to have found alternatives." Henry Kissinger (1923–2023).

Facebook

https://www.facebook.com/Daringtruths01/posts/their-hairs-stand-...

Daringtruths — Their hairs stand on end when they are... — Facebook

WEBApr 16, 2023 · 3 Apr 2021 — District Judge Paul Ayers of Bedford County Court, the Senior Vice President of the Association of Her Majesty's District Judges. GDC: Helen Falcon (MBE) lied on record. OUR DISHONEST RACIST. OUR WHITE WOMAN. BEDFORD, ENGLAND: Our semi-illiterate Freemason District Judge of our Empire of STOLEN AFFLUENCE. Our ...

A brainless, crooked, unashamedly functional semi-illiterate, and hereditary racist pure White bastard. An ultra-righteous descendant of THIEVES and owners of stolen children of poor people, including the pure Black African ancestors of our impure Black Duchess, Meghan Markle (43% Nigerian), and her impure children (<100% White) — Habakkuk.

Google: Bedford's District Judge Ayers, White Skin and Stolen Trust Fund. Before Slavery, What?

"The best opportunity of developing academically and emotional." Bedford's District Judge Paul Robert Ayers, >70, a Mason, and the Senior Vice President of the Association of Her Majesty's District Judges, 3, St Paul's Square, MK40 1SQ.

A Moron Mason approved and immortalised what his poly-educated pure White superiors and supervisors in Freemasons' LUTON authorised. HHJ Perusko studied law at Poly: Not Russell Group Second Class Alternative Education - Proverbs 17:16.

"Yes, Sir, it does her honour, but it would do nobody else honour. I have indeed not read it all. But when I take up the end of a web, and find a packthread, I do not expect to find embroidery." Dr Samuel Johnson.

BEDFORD, ENGLAND: NHS/GDC, Sue Gregory (OBE), unrelentingly lied under implied oath and/or on record—Habakkuk 1:4.

A very, very, very, dishonest pure White Officer of the Most Excellent Order of our Empire of Stolen Affluence - Habakkuk.

An indiscreetly crooked hereditary racist Officer of the Most Excellent Order of our Empire of Stolen Affluence - Habakkuk.

BEDFORD, ENGLAND: District Judge Paul Robert Ayers, >70, a Mason, and the Senior Vice President of the Association of Her Majesty's District Judges, 3, St Paul's Square, MK40 1SQ, it is not the truth that you are an ultra-righteous SAINT. You are a pure White RACIST LEECH, and the pure White ancestors of your pure White father and mother were THIEVES and owners of stolen children of poor people, including the pure Black African ancestors of Colin Powell (1937–2021) - Habakkuk.

BEDFORD, ENGLAND: District Judge Paul Robert Ayers, >70, a Mason, and the Senior Vice President of the Association of Her Majesty's District Judges, 3, St Paul's Square, MK40 1SQ, unlike PUTIN'S RUSSIA, there are no oil wells or gas fields in FREEMASONS' KEMPSTON and where your own pure White mother and father were born.

BEDFORD, ENGLAND: District Judge Paul Robert Ayers, >70, a Mason, and the Senior Vice President of the Association of Her Majesty's District Judges, 3, St Paul's Square, MK40 1SQ, our own money, NIGERIA (oil/gas), is by far more relevant to the economic survival of all your own White children, your pure White father, your pure White mother, and your pure White spouse than FREEMASONS' LUTON.

BEDFORD, ENGLAND: District Judge Paul Robert Ayers, >70, a Mason, and the Senior Vice President of the Association of Her Majesty's District Judges, 3, St Paul's Square, MK40 1SQ, the very, very, very, highly luxuriant soil of Bedfordshire yields only FOOD, and there are no gold and/or diamond mines in Bishop's Stortford. Bishop's Stortford's Brother Cecil Rhodes (1853–1902), 33rd Freemason (Scottish Rite), was a hereditary White Supremacist bastard, and an industrial-scale professional THIEF—Habakkuk.

"We shall deal with the racist bastards when get out of prison." Comrade Robert Mugabe (1924 – 2019).

BEDFORD, ENGLAND: District Judge Paul Robert Ayers, >70, a Mason, and the Senior Vice President of the Association of Her Majesty's District Judges, 3, St Paul's Square, MK40 1SQ, reasoning and vision do not have finite boundaries. The mind that the NIGERIAN, from shithole Africa, did not choose is finer than the indiscreetly institutionally RACIST LEGAL SYSTEM you served, and he has the power to use cogent facts and irrefutable evidence to irreversibly destroy you and it.

Based on cogent, irrefutable, and available evidence, the supernatural exists, and it is consistently accessible to those who stand where it can come—John 14:26. The fellow is who He says He is—John 14:6. "Jesus is the bedrock of my faith." HM (1926–2022).

BEDFORD, ENGLAND: District Judge Paul Robert Ayers, >70, a Mason, and the Senior Vice President of the Association of Her Majesty's District Judges, 3, St Paul's Square, MK40 1SQ., you are worthy only because you are pure White and England is very, very, very, rich (the 6th largest economy on earth), apart from those, you are PURIFIED NOTHING.

"Affluence is not a birthright." Lord Cameron.

BEDFORD, ENGLAND: District Judge Paul Robert Ayers, >70, a Mason, and the Senior Vice President of the Association of Her Majesty's District Judges, 3, St Paul's Square, MK40 1SQ., it is absolutely impossible for your Christ-given talents and yields of the very, very, very, highly luxuriant soil on which your own pure White father and mother were born to sustain your very, very, very, high standard of living. The pure White ancestors of your own pure White father and mother were THIEVES and owners of stolen children of poor people, including the pure Black African ancestors of our impure Black Duchess, Meghan Markle (43% Nigerian), and her impure children (<100% White).

No brain. Unlike Putin's Russia, poor natural resources. Several continuous centuries of stealing and slavery preceded the huge stolen trust fund.

Google: Bedford's District Judge Ayers, White Skin and Stolen Trust Fund. Before Slavery, What?

OYINBO OMO OLE: THIEVES—HABAKKUK.

BEDFORD, ENGLAND: District Judge Paul Robert Ayers, >70, a Mason, and the Senior Vice President of the Association of Her Majesty's District Judges, 3, St Paul's Square, MK40 1SQ, then all Judges were pure White, and nearly all of them were FREEMASONS, and some of them were thicker than a gross of planks.

BEDFORD, ENGLAND: NHS/GDC, Sue Gregory (OBE) unrelentingly lied under oath and/or on record—Habakkuk 1:4.

https://www.youtube.com/watch?v=BlpH4hG7m1A.

A very, very, very, dishonest pure White member of the Most Excellent Order of our Empire of Stolen Affluence.

A crooked closeted hereditary racist pure White Officer of the Most Excellent Order of our Empire of Stolen Affluence and alleged vulgarly charitable Rotarian (Freemasonry without voodoo and/or occultists' rituals).

Just like our Universe, our Empire did not evolve from NOTHING; then, almost everything was actively and deliberately stolen with guns—Habakkuk.

The Defender of our own Faith, only our own Faith—John 14:6, should give us the tool, WE SHALL use the sword of truth, not Jonathan Aitken's, but the Divine Sword of truth that is aligned to John 14:6, to uncover, and irreversibly destroy the centuries-old, crooked, closeted hereditary white supremacist, vulgarly charitable, and Antichrist SATANIC MUMBO JUMBO of vulgarly charitable and hereditary White Supremacist Freemasons: Mediocre Mafia, New Pharisees, New Good Samaritans (Luke 10:25–37), New Good Shepherd (John 10:11–18), New God (deluded, conceited, shallow and narrow half-educated school dropouts, and MF, and their superiors who wear vulgar pharisees' charitable works as cloaks of deceit, and use very, very, very, expensive colourful aprons, with vulgar embroideries, to decorate the temples of their powerless and useless fertility tools, and lie that they don't lie—Psalm 53) deceive their own mentally gentler children and the imbeciles they shepherd that only they and God Almighty are truly good—Mark 10:18, integrity, friendship, respect and charity—all for one, and one for all—Habakkuk 1:4), Defenders of Faiths, including all the motley assemblies of exotic faiths and religions associated with the 15 Holy Books in the House of Commons, and Dissenters of the Faith—John 14:6).

Vulgarly charitable Freemasons are demigods, but they are not our God.

How many charitable works did Freemasons do before Slavery?

Then, theirs was not a good deal, and it remains a bad deal—Matthew 4:9.

**NINETEEN:** They have unbounded and unaccountable power to do RACIST EVIL. They hate us, and we know.

"Those who have the power to do wrong with impunity seldom wait long for the well." Dr Samuel Johnson (1709–1784).

UK justice system is racist, suggests one of Britain's only ... UK justice system is racist, suggests one of Britain's only ...

10 Jan 2017—Britain's justice system is racist and should not be trusted by ethnic minorities, one of the UK's only black judges has suggested.
The Independent
https://www.independent.co.uk › UK › Home News.

"Prince Charles news: Why Prince Charles would choose NOT to become Defender of the Faith. PRINCE CHARLES will become the next King of England and is currently the oldest King in Waiting in history at 71, having spent nearly his entire life as first-in-line. When he does succeed Queen Elizabeth II, however, he said he would drop one of the monarchy's core mottos. Prince Charles would become King Charles III when he succeeds his mother according to royal tradition and would take on all of the monarch's duties. While he would have to continue her work in the most part, he may also choose to make some alterations to his reign. In the past, the Duke of Cornwall has expressed his desire to change the wording of his future position. The monarch possesses a litany of titles when they accede the British throne. The Queen's full title is currently "Elizabeth the Second, by the Grace of God, of the United Kingdom of Great Britain and Northern Ireland and of Her other Realms and Territories Queen, Head of the Commonwealth, Defender of the Faith". When Prince Charles eventually takes her position, he will inherit those titles, but he has voiced his intention to change the "Defender of the Faith" moniker. Bestowed on King Henry VIII in 1517 by the Pope, it reflects the monarch's position as supreme governor of the Church of England. Prince Charles news: Why Prince Charles would choose NOT to become Defender of the Faith. Prince Charles news: Prince Charles may be known simply as "Defender of Faith". As such, it relates to their ability to preserve the national faith, which, since Henry VIII's rule is Christianity. However, in the more than 500 years since the title came into being, the UK's religious landscape has markedly diversified. The new interfaith identity of the country has led Prince Charles to voice his preference for the streamlined "Defender of Faith" instead. He revealed his intentions in 2008, in a bid to add a contemporary spin to the monarchy. Prince Charles news: British monarchs are all known as "Defender of the Faith". University College London's Constitution Unit said the move showed support for religious freedom. They said: "Charles was making the point that, in a country with many religions now present, the sovereign should be concerned to see all religion defended and not just the Church of England. "Because Latin has no definite article, he offered 'Defender of Faith' as an alternative and viable translation to signify how a sovereign should nowadays understand the contemporary meaning of the title. "In practice, religion is protected by laws made by Parliament or as a result of international agreements like the European Convention on Human Rights." Liam Doyle, 2020.

If pure white supremacist Cambridge University educated rich man's son, Sir, Mr. Justice Haddon-Cave, KC, KBE, alleged Freemason, and all the Closeted Hereditary White Supremacist Freemason Judges in Great Britain, and all the Freemasons at the Masonic Hall, New York City, 71 W 23rd Street #1003, New York, NY 10010, United States, and all the Freemasons at Clifton Masonic Hall, 1496 Van Houten Avenue, Clifton, NJ 07013, United States, and all the Freemasons at The House of the Temple, 1733 16th Street NW Town or City Washington, D.C, United States, and all the Freemasons at the Masonic Lodge, Holly Wood Forever Cemetery, 5970 Santa Monica Boulevard, Los Angeles, CA 90038, United States, and all the 33rd Degree Freemasons at The Masonic Hall, Rising Sun, 1 Mill Road, Wellingborough NN8 1PE, and all the Freemasons at The Acacia Rooms, 27 Rockingham Road, Corby NN17 1AD, and all the Freemasons at Hotspur Lodge №1626, Fern Avenue Masonic Hall, 75–83 Fern Ave, Jesmond, Newcastle upon Tyne NE2 2RA, and all the Freemasons at Kings College School Lodge, Southside Common, London SW19 4TT, and all the members of the Bedfordshire Masonic Centre, the Keep, Bedford Road, Kempston, MK42 8AH, and all the members of Freemasons' Hall, Sheaf Close, Northampton NN5 7UL, and all the members of Towcester Masonic Centre, Northampton Road, Towcester, NN12 6LD, Northamptonshire, and all the 33rd Degree Freemasons (Scottish Rite) at Freemasons' Hall, 96 George Street, Edinburgh EH2 3DH, and all the 33rd Degree Freemasons (Scottish Rite) at the Provincial Lodge

of Glasgow, 54 Berkeley Street, Glasgow G3 7DS, all the
33rd Degree Masons (Scottish Rite), at the Mother Temple,
the Grand Masonic Lodge, 60 Great Queen St, London
WC2B 5AZ, could disprove the truth, which is that AI
recklessly and incompetently lied on record (immortal
mendacity), and if they could disprove the truth, which is
that which is that pure White Victoria Harrison, NHS
Consultant, Northamptonshire PCT, unrelentingly lied
under implied oath and/or record, or she was pathologically
confused (Alzheimer's disease), and if they could disprove
the truth, which is that which is that OXFORD,
ENGLAND: NHS/GDCD/MPS/BDA, Pure White British
Soldier, Territorial Defence, Stephanie Twidale (TD),
unrelentingly lied under oath—Habakkuk 1:4, and if they
could disprove the truth, which is that Pure White Kevin
Atkinson, dentist, Scottish Kev, Sterling Kev, Morcott
Parish Councillor, alleged Freemason, and England's Class
Scottish Postgraduate Tutor, Oxford, unrelentingly LIED
under oath- Habakkuk 1:4, and if they could disprove the
truth, which is that GDC/NHS, Freemason, Brother,
Richard William Hill (NHS Postgraduate Tutor), fabricated
reports and unrelentingly lied under oath—Habakkuk 1:4,
a very, very, dishonest white man, a closeted hereditary
white supremacist NHS Postgraduate Tutor of our Empire
of Stolen Affluence—Habakkuk, they will confirm the
belief of all Freemasons in the world, which is that very,
very, Charitable, Antichrist Freemasonry Quasi-Religion
(Mediocre Mafia, New Pharisees, New Good Samaritans
(Luke 10: 25–37), New Good Shepherd (John 10: 11- 18),
New God, Defenders of Faiths, including all the motley
assemblies of exotic faiths and religions associated with the

15 Holy Books in the House of Commons, and Dissenters of the Faith—John 14:6) is not an intellectually flawed SATANIC MUMBO JUMBO—centuries-old closeted hereditary white supremacists' scam, and they will confirm the belief of Dissenters of the Faith (John 14:6), which is that reasoning and vision have finite boundaries, and if reasoning and vision have finite boundaries, the fellow must have LIED, in the Council, before Romans and Jews, when He, purportedly, disclosed pictures His unbounded painted, and He must have also lied when He audaciously stated that He was Divinely Extra-ordinarily Exceptional—John 14:6. If the fellow told Jews and Romans the truth—in the Council, we are all FORKED, as His Knights attack all Kings and Queens simultaneously, and only Queens can escape, and everything that is not aligned with the exceptionalism of the fellow (John 14:6)—is irreversibly doomed and heading straight for the ROCK.

"It does no harm to throw the occasional man overboard, but it does not do much good if you are steering full speed ahead for the rocks." Sir Ian Gilmour (1926–2007).

Facts are sacred, and they cannot be overstated. "The truth allows no choice." Dr Samuel Johnson.

medium.com

https://yinkabamgbelu441.medium.com/nigeria-shells-cash-cow-e7…

NIGERIA: SHELL'S CASH COW.—
yinkabamgbelu441.medium.com

WEBApr 15, 2021 · DISTRICT JUDGE AYERS OF BEDFORD COUNTY COURT: A BRAINLESS WHITE MAN; A RACIST DESCENDANT OF PROFESSIONAL THIEVES AND … The Law Paralysed by Michael Coleade—YouTube. https://www.youtube.com › watch. 2:05. Sir Winston Churchill Based on accessible information, it is the absolute truth that District …

**TWENTY:** 'Scotland, about six million, mostly overfed, and overweight pure White fools (predominantly but not exclusively pure White)." Thomas Carlyle (1795–1881) paraphrased.

A brainless hereditary racist pure White bastard ultra-righteously sat on a very, very, very, expensive highchair that the imbeciles who sat before him couldn't and didn't buy, in our Grand Cathedral Court that was preceded by SLAVERY, future flats, and absolutely inevitable distant future nuclear ash.

BEDFORD, ENGLAND: District Judge Paul Robert Ayers, >70, a Mason, and the Senior Vice President of the Association of Her Majesty's District Judges, 3, St Paul's Square, MK40 1SQ, immodesty apart, you're inferiorly created by Almighty God, and it is absolutely impossible to use cogent facts and irrefutable evidence to disprove that truth.

BEDFORD, ENGLAND: District Judge Paul Robert Ayers, >70, a Mason, and the Senior Vice President of the Association of Her Majesty's District Judges, 3, St Paul's Square, MK40 1SQ, the NIGERIAN, from shithole Africa, does not see you as you see yourself, and he does not see you as imbeciles you shepherd see you, she sees you as you truly are.

YOU ARE PURIFIED FROTH.

Apart from your 5th Rate Poly Law Degree, you owe absolutely everything else to FREEMASONS' PATRONAGE.

They hate us, and we know. The only BLACK they truly love is our own shithole Africa's money (natural resources and raw materials).

YOUR MAJESTY, FREEMASONS ARE EVERYWHERE IN GREAT BRITAIN, AND THEY CONTROL ALMOST EVERYTHING, AND THEY ARE A PROPERLY ORGANISED GANG OF RACIST CRIMINALS – HABAKKUK 1:4.

BEDFORD, ENGLAND: NHS/GDC, Freemason, Brother, Richard William Hill, Senior NHS Postgraduate Tutor, Bedfordshire, fabricated reports and unrelentingly lied under oath—Habakkuk 1:4

DO FREEMASONS GUIDE AND GUARD RACIAL HATRED AND FRAUD?

BEDFORD, ENGLAND: District Judge, the SUPERNATURAL exists, and it is consistently accessible to those who stand where it can come—John 14:26, and it possible to use that supernatural truth to irreversibly destroy you, and the indiscreetly racist, and unashamedly mediocre legal system that you served—Habakkuk 1:4.

You are an opportunist racist bastard, and a spineless pure White thug, with a great snout. Then, in the dormitories at Anglican Church Grammar School, your type were taught unforgettable lessons.

"We shall deal with the racist bastards when we get out of prison." Comrade Robert Mugabe (1924 – 2019).

Google: Bedford's District Judge, White Skin and Stolen Trust Fund. Before Slavery, What?

A brainless opportunist racist pure White bastard, a mere plebeian poly-educated former debt-collector Solicitor in Norwich (5th Rate Partner), rode a very, very, very, powerful tiger, and deluded, he thought he was a very, very, very, powerful tiger, dismounted, the MF son of a hoe will instantly revert to NOTHING. Perception is grander than reality.

Like his mentally gentler White children, the imbeciles who sat before him, in our own Grand Cathedral Court that was preceded by SLAVERY, didn't know that his nomination and constructive appointment as a Judge by DEMENTING or DEMENTED (Alzheimer's disease) pure White hereditary White Supremacist Freemason Judges— was not based on progressive, colour-blind, and measurable objectivity, and they did not know that the last time the very, very, very, hardened opportunist racist pure White bastard passed through a filter of measurable objectivity was when the hereditary White supremacist thug studied 5th Rate Law at Poly (not Russell Group Lower-Class Alternative Education—Proverbs 17:16), and it showed.

Then, Alzheimer's disease was not uncommon in their House of Lords, and it was incompatible with the competent administration of the Law.

The competent administration of English Law should be an inviolable basic right.

"Freedom of expression is a basic right." Lady Hale.

"This man I thought had been a Lord of wits, but I find he is only wit among Lords." Dr Samuel Johnson.

Then, all Judges were pure White, and most of them were FREEMASONS, and some of them are thicker than a gross of planks.

"Should 500 men, ordinary men, chosen accidentally from among the unemployed, override the judgement—the deliberate judgement—of millions of people who are engaged in the industry which makes the wealth of the country?" David Lloyd George (1863–1945).

BEDFORD, ENGLAND: District Judge Paul Robert Ayers, >70, a Mason, and the Senior Vice President of the Association of Her Majesty's District Judges, 3, St Paul's Square, MK40 1SQ, a brainless racist pure White bastard wants SUPERIORITY, his baseless and brainless inviolable birth right, and he can have it, but only based on colour-blind and measurable objectivity, and what's wrong with that?

Your Majesty, the defender of our own faith, the faith—John 14:6: Defenders of Faiths (Freemasons) are Dissenters of the Faith—John 14:6, and the enemies of our own Messiah are the enemies of the Defender of our own Faith, the Faith—John 14:6.

They are a properly organised gang of RACIST CRIMINALS, and they are omnipresent, as their people are everywhere, and they control almost everything in their country.

BEDFORD, ENGLAND: District Judge Paul Robert Ayers, >70, a Mason, and the Senior Vice President of the Association of Her Majesty's District Judges, 3, St Paul's Square, MK40 1SQ.

A brainless racist pure White bastard: The only evidence of his Higher IQ is the STOLEN AFFLUENCE that his thoroughly wretched pure White ancestors crossed the English Channels, without luggage or decent shoes, to latch onto. They arbitrarily acquired camouflage English names and blended with yields of several continuous centuries of merciless RACIST EVIL: The nastiest racist terrorism and greediest economic cannibalism the world will ever know—Habakkuk.

An ignorant LEECH. An ultra-righteous descendant of THIEVES and owners of stolen children of poor people - Habakkuk. No brain. Unlike Putin's Russia, there are no oil wells or gas fields in LUTON and where his own pure White father and mother were born.

Ignorance is bliss.

"Those who know the least obey the best." George Farquhar (1677–1707).

OYINBO OMO OLE: THIEVES—HABAKKUK.

OXFORD, ENGLAND: NHS/GDC, Mrs Helen Falcon (MBE), Member of GDC Committee (former), a mere dmf, a vulgarly charitable Rotarian (Freemasonry without voodoo and/or occultists' rituals), our Postgraduate Dean, Oxford (former), and the spouse of Mr Falcon, unrelentingly lied under oath and/or on record—Habakkuk 1:4.

A very, very, very, DISHONEST pure White cougar. A crooked closeted hereditary racist Member of the Most Excellent of our Empire of Stolen Affluence—Habakkuk.

The entire foundation of Bristol, including Bristol University, where the homunculus crooked racist cougar studied dmf, was built on BONES, bones of stolen children of poor people, including the pure Black African ancestors of our impure Black Duchess, Meghan Markle (43% Nigerian), and her impure children (<100% White), and more bones than the millions of skulls at the doorstep of Comrade Pol Pot (1925–1998).

 An ignorant ultra-righteous descendant of THIEVES (OYINBO OLE) and owners of stolen children of poor people, including the pure Black African ancestors of the impure (<100% White) great grandchildren of the Duke of Edinburgh, of blessed memory, Prince Phillip (1921–2021).

 Philippians 1:21: Phillip was a 33rd Degree Freemason (Scottish Rite).

They are very, very, very, highly civilised, and super-enlightened, and they do everything legally, including RACIAL HATRED and FRAUD: Rules-based procedure, precedent, and statute etcetera.

Medium

https://medium.com/@cole69915/jews-are-very-good-with-money-a...

"JEWS ARE VERY GOOD WITH MONEY."—Medium

WEBAug 22, 2022 · District Judge Ayers, Bedford. Freemasons teach members secret handshakes, not grammar. GDC: Richard Hill fabricated reports and unrelentingly lied under oath. GDC: Kevin Atkinson (NHS …

37, Wimpole Street, W1G 8DQ: "I nearly cried at my desk." Jonathan Martin, GDC Manager (Casework), 1 Colmore Square, B4 6AA. Poly-educated hereditary racist pure White rubbish was granted the platform to display hereditary prejudice.

Indian Dentist, Dr Anand Kamath, only 42, did not nearly die.

Google: Dr Anand Kamath, Dentist.

Nigerian General Practitioner, Richard Bamgboye, only 56, did not nearly die.

Google: Dr Richard Bamgboye, GP.

Just like Alexei Navalny, only 47, Anand Kamath, only 42, and Richard Bamgboye, only 56, did not die naturally, they were mercilessly KILLED by extremely nasty RACIST BASTARDS, albeit hands-off, with the mens rea hidden in the belly of the actus reus.

They kill foreigners, and only foreigners, not because merciless EVIL is in the interest of the British public, they kill our people solely to bury RACIST EVIL.

They are trying to kill another Nigerian, from shithole Africa, because he knows that they are a properly organised gang of RACIST CRIMINALS and EVIL KILLERS, and he has evidence, so they seek to tie all loose ends by switching off all victims and/or witnesses of merciless RACIST EVIL.

OXFORD, ENGLAND: GDC/NHS, Mrs Helen Falcon (MBE), Member of GDC Committee (former), vulgarly charitable ROTARIAN (Freemasonry without voodoo and/or occultists' rituals), a mere dmf, our Postgraduate Dean, Oxford, and the spouse of Mr Falcon, unrelentingly lied under oath and/or on record - Habakkuk 1:4.

A very, very, very, dishonest pure White cougar. A crooked closeted hereditary racist Member of the Most Excellent Order of our Empire of Stolen Affluence - Habakkuk.

The entire foundation of their civilisation is RACIAL HATRED and FRAUD.

An ignorant ultra-righteous descendant of THIEVES and owners of stolen children of poor people, including the pure Black African ancestors of our impure Black Duchess, Meghan Markle (43% Nigerian), and her impure children (<100% White).

Mrs Helen Falcon (MBE), Member of GDC Committee (former), vulgarly charitable ROTARIAN (Freemasonry without voodoo and/or occultists' rituals), a mere dmf, our Postgraduate Dean, Oxford, and the spouse of Mr Falcon, pure White cougar, let me tell you, the entire foundation of Bristol, including Bristol University where you studied mere dmf, was built on foundation of BONES, more bones than the millions of skulls at the doorstep of Comrade Pol Pot (1925–1998).

"The white man is the devil." Elijah Mohammed (1897–1975).

Based on several decades of very, very, very, proximate observations and direct experiences, a White man is not only a devil, but he is also a THIEF, and he is thoroughly crazy.

SCOTLAND, A MERE QUASI-PROVINCE OF ENGLAND: GDC/NHS, Kevin Atkinson, Scottish Kev, Sterling Kev, Dentist Little Glasgow (Corby), England's Class Scottish Postgraduate Tutor, Oxford, with ZERO tangible postgraduate qualification, Councillor Morcott Parish, and the spouse of Annie, unrelentingly lied under oath-Habakkuk 1:4.

A very, very, very, DISHONEST pure White Scotchman. A crooked closeted hereditary racist Councillor Morcott Parish. The pure White Scottish ancestors of his pure White Scottish father and mother were incompetent RACIST LIARS too, they were THIEVES and owners of stolen children of poor people, including the pure Black African ancestors of the impure White (<100% White) great grandchildren of the Duke of Edinburgh, of blessed memory, Prince Phillip (1921–2021).

Philippians 1:21: Phillip was a 33rd Degree FREEMASON (Scottish Rite).

He is watching them-Proverbs 15:3.

The nemesis is not extinct, and the fact that it tarries isn't proof that it will never come - Habakkuk.

"Many Scot masters were considered among the most brutal, with life expectancy on their plantations averaging a mere four years. We worked them to death then simply imported more to keep the sugar and thus the money flowing. Unlike centuries of grief and murder, an apology cost nothing. So, what does Scotland have to say?" Herald Scotland: Ian Bell, Columnist, Sunday 28 April 2013.

If there are cogent and irrefutable evidence that the pure White Scottish ancestors of the pure White Scottish father and mother of pure White Scottish Kevin Atkinson, Scottish Kev, Sterling Kev, Dentist Little Glasgow (Corby), England's Class Scottish Postgraduate Tutor, Oxford, with ZERO tangible postgraduate qualification, Councillor Morcott Parish, and the spouse of Annie, were THIEVES (Habakkuk): Extremely nasty, and merciless, RACIST MURDERERS and owners of stolen children of defenceless poor people, it would be very, very, very, naive not to expect RACIAL HATRED complicated by incompetent mendacity, to be part of the genetic inheritances of the crooked hereditary racist pure White Scottish bastard.

Mrs Helen Falcon, Member of the Most Excellent Order of our Empire instructed the hereditary RACIST Scottish crook (Kevin Atkinson), and those who nominated, appointed, and instructed Mrs Helen Falcon (MBE) paid the salaries of all Judges: Conflict of interest in creeping DPRK.
Medium

https://medium.com/@yinkabamgbelu45/based-on-available-eviden…

Based on available evidence, Sue Gregory (OBE), Officer of the …

WEBOct 29, 2021 · district judge ayers of bedford county court: a brainless white man; a racist descendant of professional thieves and … Daringtruths-Posts | Facebookwww. facebook.com › Daringtruths01 …

Gigantic yields of millions of stolen children of defenceless poor people, including the pure Black African ancestors of our impure Black Duchess, Meghan Markle (43% Nigerian), and her impure children (<100% White), not feudal agriculture lured the Jewish ancestors of Benjamin Disraeli (1804–1881) to Great Britain. Before Slavery, what? Which part of our own shithole Africa is great? "How Europe underdeveloped Africa." Dr Walter Rodney (1942–1980)

**TWENTY-ONE:** If we aren't very, very, very, smart, why are we the sixth largest economy in the world? Shepherds did not bring stolen children back home, they sold stolen children of poor people elsewhere, and the LIED to their moron sheep that they were paragons of vision, wisdom, and virtue who, like Mother Teresa of Calcutta, did only very, very, very, good works in AFRICA.

"Someone must be trusted. Let it be the Judges." Lord Denning (1899–1999).

Judges are human beings: Some human beings are racists.

No one is good, not even one—Psalm 53.

"All sections of UK society are institutionally racist.

The Judiciary is part of UK society.

Based on several decades of very, very, very, proximate observations and direct experiences, there is no law in their country: Their law is what FREEMASON JUDGES want.

Facts are sacred, and they cannot be overstated.

Archie is impure (<100% White).

Prior to SLAVERY, there weren't very many proper houses in BEDFORD. Then, there was only subsistence feudal agriculture.

"Agriculture not only gives riches to a nation, but the oil one she can call her own." Dr Samuel Johnson (1709–1784).

A GENETIC PURE WHITE THIEF.

"The best opportunity of developing academically and emotional." Bedford Paul Robert Ayers, >70, a Mason, and the Senior Vice President of the Association of Her Majesty's District Judges, 3, St Paul's Square, MK40 1SQ.

A brainless racist pure White bastard, an ignorant ultra-righteous descendant of THIEVES and owners of stolen children of poor people, including the pure Black African ancestors of Kamala Harris, approved and immortalised what his own pure White father and mother spoke, the type of stories his pure White father used to tell when he returned home from his regular pub crawl (Nag's Head, Queen Victoria, Greene King etcetera), at very, very, very, odd hours, thoroughly stoned, angry, hungry, and very, very, very, RANDY, which his poly-educated pure White superiors and supervisors in LUTON authorised.

**HHJ Perusko studied law at Poly: Not Russell Group Second Class Alternative Education—Proverbs 17:16.**

"To survive, you must tell stories. ... I believe that what we become depends on what our fathers teach us at odd moments, when they aren't trying to teach us. We are formed by little scraps of wisdom." Umberto Eco (1932–2016).

Saxe-Coburg, and Gotha, family crossed the English Channels.

Ali Kemal (1869–1922) crossed the English Channel in 1909.

Mustafa Mehmet is Turkish, but Boris Johnson isn't.

The real name of Ghislaine Maxwell's dad was Ján Ludvík Hyman Binyamin Hoch, and he came from Czechoslovakia in the 40s.

BEDFORD, ENGLAND: District Judge Paul Robert Ayers, >70, a Mason, and the Senior Vice President of the Association of Her Majesty's District Judges, 3, St Paul's Square, MK40 1SQ, what is the real name of your own father, where did he come from, and when? Did the pure White ancestors of your own pure White father and mother evolve from black monkeys with tails to tailless white monkeys in the Epping Forest? Ignorance is bliss.

"The supreme vice is shallowness." Wilde.

A brainless racist pure White bastard ultra-righteously sat on bones of stolen children of poor people, including the pure Black African ancestors of our impure Black Duchess, Meghan Markle(43% Nigerian),and her impure children(<100% White), and more bones than the millions of skulls at the doorstep of Comrade Pol Pot (1925–1998), in our Grand Cathedral Court that was preceded by SLAVERY, future flats.

29, Goldington Road, MK 40 3NN is a block of flats.

Brainless hereditary racist pure White bastards (predominantly but not exclusively pure White) love superiority, their brainless and baseless birth right, but they hate FREEDOM OF EXPRESSION because they don't want their mentally gentler children and the imbeciles they shepherd to know the truth.

Their hairs stand of end when they are challenged by self-educated NIGERIANS, from shithole Africa; we and our type are the ones RACIST BASTARDS would beat up without the support of the YANKS. If FREEMASONS are quasi-voodoo men, occultists and ritualists as they seem to brag, they should use voodoo to evict Putin from Crimea, he stole it with guns.

Your Majesty, very, very, charitable, Antichrist closeted hereditary white supremacist Freemasons are showing your (John 14:6 Christian) African subjects—PEPPER, and we hate PEPPER SOUP.

Give us the tools (President Thomas Jefferson's level of FREEDOM OF EXPRESSION), and we shall deal closeted hereditary white supremacist bastards. We know things about them—they don't want the public to know about.

They are thoroughly crazy lunatics with ENORMOUS unbounded, unaccountable, and illegal usurped power, and they have informal access to very, very, very, powerful pure white Freemason Judges—Habakkuk 1:4.

Racial hatred is not a myth, and it is not extinct, and it is considerably more common than ordinarily realised.

BEDFORD, ENGLAND: District Judge Paul Robert Ayers, >70, a Mason, and the Senior Vice President of the Association of Her Majesty's District Judges, 3, St Paul's Square, MK40 1SQ,, the mind that the NIGERIAN, from shithole Africa did not choose, is finer than the LEGAL SYSTEM you served, and he does not believe any part of it, as no part of it is good, not even one—Psalm 53, and he has the power to use cogent facts and irrefutable evidence to irreversibly destroy you and it.

Reasoning and vision do not have finite boundaries. The supernatural exists and it is consistently accessible to those who stand where it can come—John 14:26.

The fellow is who He says He is—John 14:6. "Jesus is the bedrock of my faith." HM (1926–2022).

"The White man is the devil." Brother Mohammed Ali (1942–2016).

Based on several decades of very, very, very, proximate observations and direct experiences, a White man is not only a devil, but he is also a THIEF, and he is thoroughly crazy.

They want brainless and baseless superiority, but they don't want Freedom of Expression because they don't want their mentally gentler children and the imbeciles they shepherd to know the truth - Habakkuk 1:4.

"Freedom of Expression is basic right" Lady Hale.

Based on several decades of very, very, very, proximate observations and direct experiences, they want everything, and to eat all their own cakes and have them, and to eat all our own cakes and have them - Habakkuk 2:5.

Based on several decades of very, very, very, proximate observations and direct experiences, they are nastier than Yevgeny Prigozhin (1961–2023), and greedier than the grave, and like death, the insatiably greedy racist bastards will never be satisfied—Habakkuk 2:5.

## OYINBO OMO OLE: THIEVES—HABAKKUK.

Just as it was in Professor Stephen Hawking's School, then, at the University of Lagos, the brightest students did Mathematics, Physics, and chemistry, and did not attend lectures at the Faculty of Law.

"In my school, the brightest boys did math and physics, the less bright did physics and chemistry, and the least bright did biology. I wanted to do math and physics, but my father made me do chemistry because he thought there would be no jobs for mathematicians." Dr Stephen Hawking (1942–2018).

Based on several decades of very, very, very, proximate observations, and direct experiences, they are grossly overrated, overhyped, overpopulated, and mediocre trade that is dying slowly and imperceptibly, and is overseen by the Antichrist Racist Freemasons (Mediocre Mafia, New Pharisees, New Good Samaritans (Luke 10:25–37), New Good Shepherd (John 10: 11- 18), New God (deluded and conceited closeted hereditary RACIST pure White supremacist bastards seem to believe that only they and Almighty God are truly good—Mark 10:18; integrity, friendship, respect, and charity—all for one, and one for all—Habakkuk 1:4, defenders of Faiths, including the motley assemblies of exotic religions and faiths associated with the 15 Holy Book in the House of Commons, and dissenters of the faith—John 14:6).

Very, very, very, hardened hereditary racist incompetent liars—Habakkuk 1:4; John 8:44; John 10:10.

"The legal system lies at the heart of any society, protecting rights, imposing duties, and establishing a framework for the conduct of almost every social, political, and economic activity. Some argue that the law is in its death throes while others postulate a contrary prognosis that discerns numerous signs of law's enduring strength. Which is it?" Professor Raymond Wacks.

Racist pure White bastards (predominantly but not exclusively pure White) persecute our people for the dark coat we neither made nor chose, and cannot change, and instead of paying equitably just reparation, and settle several centuries of accruing interest, they steal yields of our Christ's granted talents, and they impede our ascent from the bottomless crater into which their very, very, greedy racist bastard ancestors—threw ours, in the African bush, unprovoked, during several continuous centuries of merciless racist evil: The evilest economic cannibalism and the greediest racist terrorism the world will ever know—Habakkuk.

OYINBO OMO OLE: THIEVES—HABAKKUK.

Facts are sacred, and they cannot be overstated.

Which one of our putrid tubes did our Born-Again informally tell Bedford's Freemason District Judge and Freemasons at Brickhill Baptist Church she used to work for £0.5M?

She pays tithe (quasi-protection money), and prays to CHRIST at Brickhill Baptist Church, Bedford, and Antichrist Freemasons in Kempston answers—all her prayers.

They saw two holes, Hypothyroidism Psychosis and Religious Psychosis, and they seek to use them to destroy the futures of pure Black NIGERIAN children.

Our Duchess, Meghan Markle is impure Black (43% Nigerian). "Meghan Markle was the victim of explicit and obnoxious racial hatred." John Bercow, a former speaker.

2 Thessalonians 3:6–10: Then, everyone was white, and white Judges sent their own white daughter to universities, so that they can gain qualifications, and their eat their own FOOD, but they also sent there to use their putrid tubes to ensnare men who would pay them for pleasurable insertions—Quasi-Hoes.

Facebook

https://www.facebook.com/Daringtruths01/posts/41851266749452...

Daringtruths—A RACIST. BEDFORD: DISTRICT JUDGE. A…—Facebook

WEBAug 12, 2022 · JUDGE PAUL AYERS, prior to the European commerce in STOLEN HUMAN BEINGS, there weren't very many proper houses in BEDFORD. In that era, JUDGES like you were complicit in MERCILESS RACIST EVIL (SLAVERY); they were fed like battery hens with its yields. Founded: 15/08/2018. Daringtruths—England is a scam Daringtruths—

**TWENTY-TWO:** Google Mediocre GDC. Pure White Jonathan Martin, Manager at the GDC, 37, Wimpole Street, London, W1G 8DQ, nearly cried at his desk. A brainless poly-educated pure White plebeian (Archie is impure, <100 White). Only the universally acknowledged irrefutably SUPERIOR SKIN COLOUR of Jonathan Martin, Manager at the GDC, 1 Colmore Row, Birmingham, B4 6AA, and Almighty God are TRULY GOOD—Mark 10:18, and he neither made nor chose it, and he would be considerably diminished as a human being without it, and he knows it: WHITE PRIVILEGE.

Based on several decades of very, very, very, proximate observations and direct experiences, their skin colour is universally acknowledged to be irrefutably SUPERIOR, but their intellects are not, and their LEGAL SYSTEM is fundamentally designed to conceal that truth.

"They may not have been well written from a grammatical point of view but I am confident I had not forgotten any of the facts." Pure White Geraint Evans, England's Class Welsh Postgraduate Tutor, Oxford.

BEDFORD, ENGLAND: District Judge Paul Robert Ayers, >70, a Mason, and the Senior Vice President of the Association of Her Majesty's District Judges, 3, St Paul's Square, MK40 1SQ, it is not the truth that daily dialogues with pure White imbeciles (predominantly, but not exclusively pure White adults with the basic skills of a child), including Pure White Geraint Evans, England's Class Welsh Postgraduate Tutor, Oxford, and his type, is a proper job that is worthwhile and manly—Habakkuk 1:4.

Google: The White Judge Lied.

Poly-educated hereditary racist unashamedly functional semi-illiterate PURE WHITE RUBBISH rode a very, very, very, powerful tiger, and deluded, the hereditary racist pure White bastard, a mere former debt-collector Solicitor in NORWICH (5th Rate Partner), believed that he was a very, very, very, powerful tiger, dismounted, the poly-educated overpromoted plebeian (FREEMASONRY'S PATRONAGE), would instantly revert to nothing.

Abuse of temporary power is the fullest definition of evil: "The highest reach of injustice is to be deemed just when you are not." Plato.

Google: White skin and stolen trust fund. Before Slavery, what?

BEDFORD, ENGLAND: District Judge Paul Robert Ayers, >70, a Mason, and the Senior Vice President of the Association of Her Majesty's District Judges, 3, St Paul's Square, MK40 1SQ, you have a grossly exaggerated sense of self-worth. The pure White ancestors of your own pure White mother and father were THIEVES and owners of stolen children of poor people. Like the imbeciles who sat before you, your mentally gentler children did not know that your nomination and constructive appointment as our Judge by dementing or demented hereditary White Supremacist Freemason Lord—was not based on progressive, colour-blind, and measurable objectivity, and it showed, and the imbeciles you shepherd did not know that the last time you passed through a filter of measurable objectivity was when you studied 5th rate law at poly, and that showed too.

"This man I thought had been a Lord of wits, but I find he is only a wit among Lords." Dr Samuel Johnson

A brainless hereditary racist pure White bastard, the only evidence of his very, very, very, HIGH IQ, is the stolen affluence that the thoroughly wretched pure White ancestors of his pure White mother and father crossed the English Channels, not that long ago, without luggage or decent shoes, to latch onto—Habakkuk.

Medium

https://medium.com/@mluther88983/dr-richard-dawkins-then-crook...

Dr Richard Dawkins: Then, crooked closeted hereditary racist

WEBDec 28, 2023 · WebNov 18, 2023 · WebDISTRICT JUDGE PAUL AYERS, prior to the European commerce in STOLEN HUMAN BEINGS, there weren't very many proper houses in BEDFORD. In that era, JUDGES like you were ...

Ignorant ultra-righteous members of the brainless and baselessly self-awarded superior race, descendants of PURE WHITE THIEVES, see molecules and they maliciously destroy all self-educated NIGERIANS, from shithole Africa, who see quarks: Matthew 2:16.

Matthew 27: 32–56: Your Majesty, the defender of our own faith, when the builders of that era, including stonemasons, realised that our own Messiah was intellectually unplayable, He was kidnapped, and crooked charges were criminally attached to Him, and He was crookedly tried in a crooked court before a crooked Judge, and He was baselessly found guilty, and He was lynched like Gadhafi and crucified only because He spoke, He disclosed pictures His unbounded mind painted.

Your Majesty, the defender of our own faith (John 14:6), our own Messiah, the bedrock of HM's (1926–2022) faith, was not punished for speaking, the sinless transparently true Judge (John 5:22, Matthew 25: 31–46) was killed solely to prevent Him from speaking.

"Freedom of expression is the cornerstone of our democracy." The Right Honourable Jacob Rees-Mogg (MP).

Your Majesty, the defender of our own faith (John 14:6), the stone that the builders, including stonemasons of that era, rejected is now the cornerstone—Psalm 118:22, Luke 20:17.

Facts are sacred, and they cannot be overstated.

BEDFORD, ENGLAND: NHS/GDC, Freemason, Brother Richard William Hill, Senior NHS Postgraduate Tutor, Bedfordshire, fabricated reports, and unrelentingly lied under oath—Habakkuk 1:4.

A very, very, very, dishonest pure White man. A crooked closeted hereditary racist FREEMASON.

THEIR FAKE RULES BASED SYSTEM: They are, supposedly very, very, very, highly civilised, and super-enlightened, and they deceive their mentally gentler children and the IMBECILES (adults with the basic skills of a child) they shepherd that they do everything LEGALLY (rules-based procedures, precedent, and statute etcetera), but including RACIAL HATRED and FRAUD.

Based on several decades of very, very, very, proximate observations and direct experiences, they are extremely nasty RACIST CRIMINALS, and they oversee the administration of their law, and they have only one method of doing RACIST EVIL and they use it all the time: They criminally attach RACIST EVIL to Nigerians, from shithole Africa, and other foreigners who disagree with members of the brainlessly and baselessly self-awarded superior race, and they criminally do RACIAL HATRED until takes hold, and when it does, they instantly revert to LEGALITY, the legality whose entire foundation is MERCILESS RACIAL HATRED and FRAUD. Integrity, friendship, respect, and charity: All for one, and one for all. Their people are everywhere in their country, and they control almost everything, and they oversee the administration of their law.

Based on several decades of very, very, very, proximate observations and direct experiences, the pattern of merciless RACIST EVIL is the same everywhere in their country—Habakkuk 1:4.

BEDFORD, ENGLAND: NHS/GDC, Sue Gregory (OBE), alleged vulgarly charitable Rotarian (Freemasonry without voodoo and/or occultists' rituals), unrelentingly lied under implied oath and/or on record—Habakkuk 1:4.

A very, very, very, dishonest pure White cougar. A crooked closeted hereditary racist Officer of the Most Excellent Order of our Empire of Stolen Affluence — Habakkuk.

**TWENTY-THREE:** Based on several decades of very, very, very, proximate observations and direct experiences, the weapon of the privileged dullard, the direct descendant of the father of RACIST LIES (John 8:44, John 10:10) is the mother of RACIST LIES, and her power is the certainty that all Judges would be PURE WHITE, and her hope is that all Judges will be pure White racist bastards too—Habakkuk 1:4.

Based on several decades of very, very, very, proximate observations and direct experiences, theirs is irreparably bastardised, unashamedly mediocre, indiscreetly dishonest, vindictive, potently weaponised, and unapologetically institutionally racist, and it is overseen by members of the vulgarly charitable, Antichrist, and closeted hereditary White Supremacist Freemasonry Quasi-Religion (Mediocre Mafia, New Pharisees, New Good Samaritans (Luke 10: 25–37), New Good Shepherd (John 10: 11–18), New God (deluded and conceited hereditary white supremacist bastards believe that ONLY they and Almighty God are TRULY GOOD—Mark 10:18: Integrity, friendship, respect, and charity—all for one, and one for all), Defenders of Faiths, including all the motley assemblies of exotic religions and faiths associated with the 15 Holy Books in the House of Commons, and Dissenters of the Faith—John 14:6).

Based on several decades of very, very, very, proximate observations and direct experiences, they are a properly organised gang of RACIST PURE WHITE CRIMINALS, and they vindictively destroy all self-educated Nigerians, and other foreigners, who disagree with members of the baselessly and brainlessly self-awarded SUPERIOR RACE, and they criminally annul the formal education of our people, and they steal yields of our Christ granted talents, and they impede the ascent of our people from the bottomless crater in to which their very, very, very, greedy racist ancestors threw ours, in the AFRICAN BUSH, unprovoked, during several continuous centuries of merciless RACIST EVIL: The greediest economic cannibalism and the evilest racist terrorism the world will ever know—Habakkuk, and motivated by hereditary RACIAL HATRED and uncontrollable ENVY, they economically strangulate our people, and they maliciously place insurmountable obstacles before our people, and they viciously overwhelm the minds of our people, and they sadistically irreversibly damage the minds of our people, and they kill our people, albeit hands-off, with the mens rea hidden in the belly of the actus reus, and they deceive their own mentally gentler children and the imbeciles the shepherd that they were diligently performing their duties.

Google: Dr Richard Bamgboye, GP.

Google: Dr Anand Kamath, Dentist.

Only foreigners seem to be dying in their latent, but very, very, very, potent RACE WAR.

"When a stupid man is doing something he is ashamed of, he always declares that it is his duty." George Bernard Shaw (1856–1950).

Irish Catholic Joe, President Joseph Biden, and President Zelensky, want all Ukrainians to be part of our very, very, very, highly civilised, and super-enlightened free world, where pure White people, only pure White people, are allowed to fabricate reports and tell incompetent racist lies under oath, but President Putin doesn't, so he converted Avdiivka from bricks to rubble and stole it.

Your Majesty, the defender of our own faith (John 14:6), based on cogent, irrefutable, and available evidence, the supernatural exists, and it is consistently accessible to those who stand where it can come—John 14:26. It is plainly deductible that reasoning and vision do not have finite boundaries.

"The blame is his who chooses. God is blameless." Plato.

The mind that the Nigerian, from shithole Africa, did not choose is finer than this system, in its entirety, and he has the power to use cogent facts and irrefutable evidence to irreversibly destroy it.

OXFORD, ENGLAND: NHS/GDC, Mrs Helen Falcon (MBE), Member of GDC Committee (former), a mere dmf, a vulgarly charitable Rotarian (Freemasonry without voodoo and/or occultists' rituals), our Postgraduate Dean, Oxford, and the spouse of Mr Falcon, unrelentingly lied under oath and/or on record—Habakkuk 1:4.

A very, very, very, dishonest pure White cougar. A crooked closeted hereditary racist Members of the Most excellent Order of our Empire of Stolen Affluence— Habakkuk.

Having FAILED in practice, the crooked closeted hereditary RACIST pure White cougar parked her liability at the public till.

"She who could, did, and she who couldn't, taught those who passed where she failed." George Bernard Shaw paraphrased.

Based on very, very, very, proximate observations and direct experiences, there was something of the midnight about the homunculus, hereditary racist, crooked cougar, Mrs Helen Falcon, Member of the Most Excellent Order of our Empire of Stolen Affluence—Habakkuk.' Anne Widdecombe paraphrased.

Facebook

https://www.facebook.com/Daringtruths01/posts/34204955547416...

Daringtruths - Half-educated School dropouts, closeted... - Facebook

WEBNov 17, 2021 · Justice, 04/01/21. District Judge Ayers, 04/01/21. Her Honour Judge Gargan … Family; District Judge Murch Yinka Bamgbelu (Daring Truths, Non-Fiction Writer) on Twitter … twitter.com › adeadeolacole1 › status 28 Nov 2018 - JUDGE AYERS,you're a bad human being,a RACIST,and a COWARD.The JUDICIARY that made you a JUDGE isn't …

**TWENTY- FOUR:** A brainless unashamedly functional semi-illiterate hereditary racist pure White bastard. An ignorant ultra-righteous descendant of PROFESSIONAL PURE WHITE THIEVES and owners of stolen children of poor people, including the pure Black African ancestors of our impure Black Duchess, Meghan Markle (<43% Nigerian), and her impure children (<100% White). Based on several decades of very, very, very, proximate observations and direct experiences, skin colour that very, very, very, fortunate wearers neither made nor chose is universally acknowledged to be irrefutably superior, but their intellects aren't, and their indiscreetly institutionally RACIST LEGAL SYSTEM is fundamentally designed to conceal that truth. "They may not have been well written from a grammatical point of view but I am confident I had not forgotten any of the facts." Geraint Evans, England's Class Welsh Imbecile Postgraduate Tutor, Oxford.

BEDFORD, ENGLAND: District Judge Paul Robert Ayers, >70, a Mason, and the Senior Vice President of the Association of Her Majesty's District Judges, 3, St Paul's Square, MK40 1SQ, it is not the truth that daily dialogues with Geraint Evans, England's Class Welsh Imbecile Postgraduate Tutor, Oxford, and his type, is a proper job, which is worthwhile and manly.

BEDFORD, ENGLAND: District Judge Paul Robert Ayers, >70, a Mason, and the Senior Vice President of the Association of Her Majesty's District Judges, 3, St Paul's Square, MK40 1SQ, apart from creating very, very, very, cushy salaried jobs for Solicitors and Barristers who

FAILED in practice, where Britons were free to use their own money to buy services from whomsoever they want, and from wherever they want, and lecherous hereditary white supremacist bastards who have now parked their liabilities at the public till where others spend other people's money on themselves and on other people (Quasi-Communism), what do pure White imbeciles (predominantly but not exclusive pure White), Geraint Evans, England's imbecile Welsh Postgraduate Tutor, Oxford, and his type need very, very, very, expensive administration of English Law for.

BEDFORD, ENGLAND: District Judge Paul Robert Ayers, >70, a Mason, and the Senior Vice President of the Association of HHer Majesty's District Judges, 3, St Paul's Square, MK40 1SQ, the Nigerian, from shithole Africa, does not believe in any part of the LEGAL SYSTEM that you served, as no part of it is good, not even one—Psalm 53.

BEDFORD, ENGLAND: District Judge Paul Robert Ayers, >70, a Mason, and the Senior Vice President of the Association of HHer Majesty's District Judges, 3, St Paul's Square, MK40 1SQ, pure White Senior Judge, let me tell you, reasoning and vision do not have finite boundaries, and the fellow is who He says His—John 14:6. "Jesus is the bedrock of my faith." HM (1926–2022).

BEDFORD, ENGLAND: District Judge Paul Robert Ayers, >70, a Mason, and the Senior Vice President of the Association of HHer Majesty's District Judges, 3, St Paul's Square, MK40 1SQ, the Nigerian from shithole Africa is very, very, very, irreconcilable different from you, as the mind that he did not choose is finer than the LEGAL SYSTEM that you served, and he has the power to use cogent facts and irrefutable evidence to irreversibly destroy you and it.

BEDFORD, ENGLAND: District Judge Paul Robert Ayers, >70, a Mason, and the Senior Vice President of the Association of HHer Majesty's District Judges, 3, St Paul's Square, MK40 1SQ, the Nigerian from shithole Africa, is a FOETUS, not by choice, not through righteousness, and not through effort, but only through unsolicited, and undeserved kindness of Christ—Romans 11, 1 John 4:4, as what he could vividly see is clearer than dreams, visions, and prophecies—Acts 2:17.

Bi mo ba ronu ni pa Edumare, ara a si gbon riri bi oye ti nse omo tuntun, ohun ti o fe fi mi se emi ko mo, sugbon o hun da eru ba mi ni gbogbo igba.

BEDFORD, ENGLAND: NHS/GDC, Sue Gregory (OBE), alleged vulgarly charitable Rotarian (Freemasonry without voodoo and/or occultists' rituals) unrelentingly lied under implied oath and/or record—Habakkuk 1:4.

A very, very, very, dishonest pure White OBE cougar. Meghan Markle is impure (only 57% White).

A crooked closeted hereditary Racist Officer of the Most Excellent Order of our Empire of Stolen Affluence— Habakkuk.

Crooked closeted hereditary racist Sue Gregory (OBE) was not deterred by His Justice (John 5:22, Matthew 25:31–46), because she did not believe in His exceptionalism—John 14:6.

Then, very, very, very, greedy, and crooked bastards won in crooked courts before crooked Judges, but in the WAR when the Corporal flipped, He looked away, and very, very, very, greedy, and crooked bastards lost everything and more—John 5:22, Matthew 25:31–46.

He, the only sinless and transparently true Judge will Judge all, including crooked hereditary White Supremacist Freemason Judges, with the sword of truth, not Jonathan Aitken's, but the Divine Sword of Truth.

Asegbe kan ko si ni abe orun. Ase pamo paapa kosi lo ju Olodumare. Ase danu ni kan lo wa. Eni to gbon ko fura. Ifura ni oogun awon agbalagba, ifura paapa agbalagba oogun ni.

Your Majesty, vulgarly charitable, Antichrist, and hereditary White Supremacist Freemasons are showing self-educated NIGERIANS, from shithole Africa, pepper in Great Britain, and we hate pepper soup.
Facebook

https://www.facebook.com/Daringtruths01/posts/41286649472580...

[Daringtruths - BEDFORD: District Judge, you're a LEECH,... - Facebook](#)

WEBJul 21, 2022 · JUDGE PAUL AYERS, prior to the European commerce in STOLEN HUMAN BEINGS, there weren't very many proper houses in BEDFORD. In that era, JUDGES like you were complicit in MERCILESS RACIST EVIL (SLAVERY); they were fed like battery hens with its yields. Founded: 15/08/2018. Daringtruths - England is a scam Daringtruths -

**TWENTY-FIVE:** No brain. Poor natural resources. Several centuries of stealing and SLAVERY preceded the huge STOLEN TRUST FUND. "The best opportunity of developing academically and emotional." Bedford's District Judge Paul Robert Ayers, >70, a Mason, and the Senior Vice President of the Association of HHer Majesty's District Judges, 3, St Paul's Square, MK40 1SQ. A brainless opportunist racist pure White bastard. His pure White skin concealed his impure dark black brain. He approved and immortalised what his pure White father and mother spoke, which poly-educated pure White superiors and supervisors in LUTON authorised.

Google: Bedford's District Judge, White skin and stolen trust fund. Before Slavery, what?

BEDFORD, ENGLAND: District Judge Paul Robert Ayers, >70, a Mason, and the Senior Vice President of the Association of HHer Majesty's District Judges, 3, St Paul's Square, MK40 1SQ, the most important part of the matter is MONEY, and our own money, NIGERIA (oil/gas), is by far more relevant to the economic survival of all your own White children, your pure White mother, your pure White father, and your pure White spouse than Freemasons' Kempston. Unlike Putin's Russia, there are no oil wells or gas fields in LUTON and where your own pure White father and mother were born, and the very, very, very, highly luxuriant soil of Bishop's Stortford yields only FOOD. Bishop Stortford's Cecil Rhodes (1853–1902) was a RACIST pure White bastard and a PROFESSIONAL THIEF.

Facts are sacred, and they cannot be overstated.

BEDFORD, ENGLAND: NHS/GDC, Sue Gregory (OBE) unrelentingly lied under oath and/or on record—Habakkuk 1:4.

A very, very, very, dishonest pure White cougar. A crooked closeted hereditary racist Officer of the Most Excellent Order of our Empire of Stolen Affluence - Habakkuk.

Oxbridge-Educated Rich Man's Son, Sir, Mr Justice Haddon ...

Amazon UK

https://www.amazon.co.uk › Oxbridge-Educated-Justice-...

White skin, huge stolen trust fund, and what else? Before Slavery, what? A racist descendant of THIEVES— Habakkuk. Geraint Evans lied. A racist Welsh crook ...

"The best opportunity of developing academically and emotional." Bedford's District Judge Paul Robert Ayers, >70, a Mason, and the Senior Vice President of the Association of Her Majesty's District Judges, 3, St Paul's Square, MK40 1SQ.

A very, very, very, hardened Racist Pure White Bastard was granted the platform to display hereditary prejudice.

"I don't want to talk grammar. I want to talk like a Lady." George Bernard Shaw.

A brainless opportunist racist pure White bastard. An ignorant, unashamedly functional semi-illiterate, and ultra-righteous descendant of THIEVES and owners of stolen children of poor people, including the pure Black African ancestors of our impure Black Duchess, Meghan Markle (43% Nigeria), and her impure children (<100% White). Like all his mentally gentler White children, the imbeciles who sat before him, in our Grand Cathedral Court that was preceded by SLAVERY, future flats, and absolutely inevitable future nuclear ash (29, Goldington Road, MK40 3NN, is a block of flats), did not know that his nomination and constructive appointment by dementing or demented poor White Freemason Judges, was not based on progressive, measurable, and colour-blind objectivity, and they did not know that the last time the hereditary racist pure White bastard, albeit England's Class Senior Judge, Bedford's District Judge, passed through a filter of measurable objectivity was when the hereditary White Supremacist bastard studied 5th Rate Law at Poly, and it showed.

"This man I thought had been a Lord of wits, but I find he is only a wit among Lords." Dr Samuel Johnson.

Then, unlike now, there were fewer than 15 Holy Books in the House of Lords, and then, like now, Alzheimer's disease was not uncommon in the House of Lords, and it was incompatible with the competent administration of English law, and in another era, the competent administration of English Law was an inviolable basic right.

Then, all Lords were Pure White Supremacists, and nearly all them were FREEMASONS, and some of them were thicker than a gross of planks.

"Should 500 men, ordinary men, chosen accidentally from among the unemployed, override the judgement—the deliberate judgement—of millions of people who are engaged in the industry which makes the wealth of the country?" David Lloyd George (1863–1945).

Case No: 2YL06820

Bedford County Court

May House

29 Goldington Road

Bedford

MK40 3NN

Monday, 1st July 2013

B E F O R E:

DISTRICT JUDGE AYERS

DOBERN PROPERTY LIMITED

(Claimants)

v.

DR. ABIODUN OLA BAMGBELU

(Defendant)

Transcript from an Official Court Tape Recording.

Transcript prepared by:

MK Transcribing Services

29 The Concourse, Brunel Business Centre,

Bletchley, Milton Keynes, MK2 2ES

Tel: 01908–640067 Fax: 01908–365958

DX 100031 Bletchley

Official Court Tape Transcribers.

MR. PURKIS appeared on behalf of THE CLAIMANTS.

THE DEFENDANT appeared in PERSON.

PROCEEDINGS OF MONDAY, 1ST JULY 2013

Monday, 1st July 2013

DISTRICT JUDGE AYERS: Mr. Purkis, you weren't here, I know, on the last occasion representing the claimants, but we had a very long hearing concerning the lease. There's a letter from Mr. Bamgbelu dated 6th June, which I don't know whether you have seen.

MR. PURKIS: Yes, sir.

DISTRICT JUDGE AYERS: In that case it seems to me it's over to you to prove your case.

MR. PURKIS: Sir, it continues to be our case that we rely on the lease and the terms of the lease that have been put forward. On the last occasion, my understanding was that it was—in essence it was accepted by the court that those terms were likely to be terms between the parties that were entered into, and I'm referring to the lease contained in the bundle. Mr. Bamgbelu was therefore required to dispute that, in essence, by providing a copy of a lease that he said contained the appropriate terms.

DISTRICT JUDGE AYERS: What I actually said to him, and I went through this numerous times with him, was that the copy of the lease that you produced was the one at the Land Registry, it happened to be the one signed by the landlord, and he was saying that that wasn't the one that was signed by him. He said he had solicitors at the time who advised him, and pressing very hard about it, and on numerous occasions, he insisted that he wished to go back to his solicitors then and find a copy of the lease that they had that they advised him on, and to check that against the copy that you have. The letter, as you see, simply says that he doesn't accept that, and it's up to you to produce a copy signed by him. Well, the position is very very clear this afternoon. I made a very clear order on the last occasion that if he didn't produce any evidence to challenge the validity of your lease, as your lease was registered at the Land Registry, I would accept that even if he would not be in a position to challenge what that lease contained. End of story. He is stuck with that lease. All I want to do today is to hear evidence from you as to the amount outstanding.

MR. PURKIS: Thank you, sir.

MR. BAMGBELU: Am I allowed to say something, sir?

DISTRICT JUDGE AYERS: No. Do you wish to—— -

MR. BAMGBELU: It is not fair, sir.

DISTRICT JUDGE AYERS: Mr. Bamgbelu, do you wish to say anything about that particular issue?

MR. BAMGBELU: Yes, sir.

DISTRICT JUDGE AYERS: What do you wish to say?

MR. BAMGBELU: The lease that I read and signed, when you sign the lease, sir, it is exchanged. The only lease that I read and signed——-

DISTRICT JUDGE AYERS: No, Mr. Bamgbelu, let me explain this to you.

MR. BAMGBELU: That'——-

DISTRICT JUDGE AYERS: It is up to the claimants to prove their case. They have produced a copy of the lease that is registered at the Land Registry. That is a lease and they are able to prove their case on that. The fact that they have not got your copy or the copy signed by you, is neither here nor there, because the importance is the document which is registered at the Land Registry, and investigations say that it is a copy signed by the landlord which has to be placed at the Land Registry. I made that perfectly clear to you on the last occasion.

MR. BAMGBELU: That's——-

DISTRICT JUDGE AYERS: You were the one who challenged that that lease was not an accurate copy of the lease that you've signed.

MR. BAMGBELU: I did not say that, sir.

DISTRICT JUDGE AYERS: Yes, you did.

MR. BAMGBELU: I did not say that, sir.

DISTRICT JUDGE AYERS: I was here the last occasion—— -

MR. BAMGBELU: I did not say that, sir.

DISTRICT JUDGE AYERS: ———that is exactly what you said.

MR. BAMGBELU: What I said, sir, was that I am happy to accept that.

DISTRICT JUDGE AYERS: No, you weren't.

MR. BAMGBELU: I said that.

DISTRICT JUDGE AYERS: Mr. Bamgbelu, you cannot argue with me, I was here, because I was at some—— -

MR. BAMGBELU: Okay.

DISTRICT JUDGE AYERS: ———considerable length to go through that with you, because you kept saying—— -

MR. BAMGBELU: I said—— -

DISTRICT JUDGE AYERS: ———that, and I said if you accept—— -

MR. BAMGBELU: I accepted it, sir.

DISTRICT JUDGE AYERS: ———if you accept that lease as the lease, then we didn't need to go any further. You insisted on having the matter adjourned so you could go—— -

MR. BAMGBELU: I did not do that, sir.

DISTRICT JUDGE AYERS: ———and get—okay.

MR. BAMGBELU: Yes.

DISTRICT JUDGE AYERS: Well, okay, we'll disagree on that then, but I can remember full well what I said——-

MR. BAMGBELU: I have a very good memory, sir.

DISTRICT JUDGE AYERS: ———and if necessary———-

MR. BAMGBELU: As well as (Inaudible).

DISTRICT JUDGE AYERS: ———if necessary I will have the tape played back to you——-

MR. BAMGBELU: Yes, yes.

DISTRICT JUDGE AYERS: ———that's exactly what is said.

MR. BAMGBELU: Okay.

MR. PURKIS: The claim is for £320.66 service charge.

DISTRICT JUDGE AYERS: Well, you'd better, I think, call your client or Mrs. Thomas to give evidence, to deal with the issues that are outstanding.

MR. PURKIS: Certainly, sir. May I call Mrs. Thomas?

Mrs. L. Thomas

Examined by Mr. Purkis.

Q. Mrs. Thomas, you have a bundle in front of you, and I believe that if you turn to page 141, you'll see a document there that says at the top, 'Witness statement of Lisa Thomas.' Is that your witness statement?

A. That's correct.

Q. If we turn to paragraph 8 there, it says, 'In the circumstances, I respectfully ask the court to enter judgment for the amount claimed of £410.66,' then it says, 'which comprises of the court fee for issuing the claim, totalling £95, and solicitors fees on issuing of £80.' Can I confirm that those fees of £95 and £80 aren't in fact included in that £410.66?

A. No, there is an error.

DISTRICT JUDGE AYERS: Right. Before we go any further, Mr. Purkis, we'd better have your client telling me who she is.

MR. PURKIS: Very well, sir. Could you give your full name to the court?

A. My name is Mrs. Lisa Jane Thomas, I'm property manager for Residential Block Management Services, and our clients are Dobern Properties.

Q. And how long have you been managing this particular block?

A. From around December 2010 when we was instructed by the previous agents. They were the administrators.

MR. BAMGBELU: Do you have proof of that?

BEDFORD, ENGLAND: Based on cogent, irrefutable, and available evidence, Bedford's District Judge, maliciously lied, or the pure White man was pathologically recklessly confused (Alzheimer's disease), or he was otherwise DISHONEST, or he was otherwise confused when he explicitly that the Nigerian, from shithole Africa, was invited to, and took part, in the hearing of July 1, 2013, at Bedford County Court, May House, 29, Goldington Road, Bedford, MK40 3NN. Based on cogent, irrefutable and available evidence, 29, Goldington Road, Bedford, MK40 3NN, is a block of flats, and absolutely inevitable future nuclear ash.

They hate us, and we know. The pure White man, albeit England's Class Senior Judge, Bedford's District, further LIED, or the pure White man was pathologically recklessly confused (Alzheimer's disease), or he was otherwise DISHONEST, or he was otherwise confused, when he stated (implied) that the name of the Negro Defendant given to the Court by Dobern Property Limited, was the name of the Defendant on the proof-read and approved Judgement of July 1, 2013.

Google: The White Judge Lied.

Google: Incompetent Liars: Some Lawyers.

**TWENTY-SIX:** If there are cogent, irrefutable, and available evidence that the pure White ancestors of the pure White father and mother of Bedford's District Judge were THIEVES and owners of stolen children of poor people, it will be very, very, very, naive.

Then, huge yields of stolen lives of pure Black children of poor AFRICANS were used to build Grand Courts and yields of merciless RACIST EVIL paid salaries of pure White Judges who sent pure White people who stole money to Great Prisons built with yields of stolen AFRICANS.

"Sometimes people don't want to hear the truth because they don't want their illusions destroyed." Friedrich Nietzsche (1844–1900).

"From around December 2010 when we was instructed by the previous agents. They were the administrators." Our functional Semi-illiterate Pure White Mrs Lisa Thomas, England's Class Property

OUR PURE WHITE IMBECILE ENGLAND'S CLASS PROPERTY MANAGER.

Facts are sacred, and they cannot be overstated.

"The best opportunity of developing academically and emotional." Bedford's District Judge Paul Robert Ayers, >70, a Mason, and the Senior Vice President of the Association of Her Majesty's District Judges, 3, St Paul's Square, MK40 1SQ.

A brainless pure White bastard.

A MORON FREEMASON.

An ignorant ultra-righteous descendant of THIEVES and owners of stolen children of people, including the pure Black African ancestors of our impure Black Duchess, Meghan Markle (43% Nigerian), and her impure children (<100% White).

Our unashamedly functional Semi-illiterate England's Class Pure White Senior Judge: OYINBO ODE.

"I have seen evil, and it has the face of Mark Fuhrman." Johnny Cochran (1937–2005).

Based on several decades of very, very, very, proximate observations and direct experiences, a white woman is not only EVIL (Jezebel), but she is also a THIEF, and she is thoroughly crazy.

BEDFORD, ENGLAND: District Judge Paul Robert Ayers, >70, a Mason, and the Senior Vice President of the Association of HHer Majesty's District Judges, 3, St Paul's Square, MK40 1SQ, the mind that the NIGERIAN, from shithole Africa, did not choose is finer than the legal system you served, and he has the POWER to irreversibly destroy you and it.

BEDFORD, ENGLAND: District Judge Paul Robert Ayers, >70, a Mason, and the Senior Vice President of the Association of HHer Majesty's District Judges, 3, St Paul's Square, MK40 1SQ, reasoning and vision do not have finite boundaries, and the supernatural exists, and it is consistently accessible to those who stand where it can come—John 14:26, and the fellow is who He says He is—John 14:6.

"Jesus is the bedrock of my faith." HM (1926- 2022).

OXFORD, ENGLAND: NHS/GDC/BDA/MPS, Stephanie Twidale, British Soldier, Territorial Defence, unrelentingly lied under oath—Habakkuk 1:4. A very, very, very, pure White cougar. A crooked closeted hereditary RACIST British Soldier.

Based on several decades of very, very, very, proximate observations and direct experiences, dishonesty is the most important hallmark of RACIAL HATRED, and it is considerably more common in the administration of English Law than ordinarily realised.

Google: Bedford's District Judge Ayers, White Skin and Stolen. Before Slavery, what?

They are very, very, very, highly civilised, and super-enlightened, and they do everything, absolutely everything legally, including RACIAL HATRED and FRAUD: Rules-based procedures, precedent, statute etcetera.

Based on cogent, irrefutable, and available evidence, Bedford's District Judge Paul Robert Ayers, >70, a Mason, and the Senior Vice President of the Association of HHer Majesty's District Judges, 3, St Paul's Square, MK40 1SQ, unrelentingly lied under oath (approved Judgement) and/or on record.

An ignorant, ultra-righteous, and hereditary racist pure White bastard, a mere poly-educated former debt-collector

Solicitor in Norwich (5th Rate Partner) was granted the platform to display hereditary prejudice.

OUR OWN NIGERIA: SHELL'S DOCILE CASH COW SINCE 1956.

BEDFORD, ENGLAND: District Judge Paul Robert Ayers, >70, a Mason, and the Senior Vice President of the Association of HHer Majesty's District Judges, 3, St Paul's Square, MK40 1SQ, unlike Putin's Russia, there are no oil wells or gas fields in FREEMASONS' NORTHAMPTON and where your own pure White father and mother were born. You are a LEECH, and the pure White ancestors of your pure White father and mother were THIEVES and owners of stolen children of poor people, including the pure Black African ancestors of our impure Black Duchess, Meghan Markle (43% Nigerian), and her impure children (<100% White).

Pure White Bedford's District Judge Paul Robert Ayers, >70, a Mason, and the Senior Vice President of the Association of Her Majesty's District Judges, 3, St Paul's Square, MK40 1SQ, coached his own pure White kindred, Mr Purkis , to call their own Pure White Kindred, Mrs Lisa Thomas, and the England's Class Imbecile Barrister asked the supposedly impartial Judge for permission to do so. Bedford District Judge did not allow Mrs Lisa Thomas to expatiate on the ERROR, which seemingly was not part of the prior agreed verdict, probably in a SATANIC FREEMASONS' TEMPLE.

"The white man is the devil." Brother Elijah Mohammed (1897–1900)

Based on several decades of very, very, very, proximate observations and direct experiences, a White woman is not only a devil (Jezebel), but she is also a THIEF, and she is thoroughly crazy.

Then, all Judges in Great Britain were pure White, and nearly all of them were FREEMASONS, and some of them were THICKER than a gross of planks.

BEDFORD, ENGLAND: NHS/GDC, Sue Gregory (OBE) unrelentingly lied under implied oath—Habakkuk 1:4

A very, very, very, dishonest pure White cougar.

A crooked closeted hereditary racist Officer of the Most Excellent Order of our Empire of Stolen Affluence— Habakkuk.

Then, verdicts were prior agreed in FREEMASONS' TEMPLES, and in the open Court incompetent art incompetently imitated life - Habakkuk 1:4.

Then, in Great Britain, cash for questions, but not cash for Judgements, was the norm.

In our own NIGERIA, then and now, cash for Judgement is the norm.

Four, too many, hereditary racist, crooked, and scatter-head pure White bastards: Bedford's District Judge, Mrs Lisa Thomas, Stephanie Twidale (TD), and Sue Gregory (OBE). Of course, they were all White: Homogeneity in the administration of English Law is the impregnable, very, very, very, secure mask of merciless RACIST EVIL— Habakkuk 1:4.

Our own NIGERIAN BABIES with huge oil wells and gas fields near their huts eat only 1.5/day in our own NIGERIA, four, too many, very, very, very, bellyful hereditary racist, crooked, and scatter-head pure White bastards: Bedford's District Judge, Mrs Lisa Thomas, Stephanie Twidale (TD), and Sue Gregory (OBE), whose pure White mothers and fathers have never seen crude oil, and whose pure White ancestors, including the pure White Welsh ancestors of Aneurin Bevan (1897–1960), were fed like battery hens with yields of stolen children of poor people, including the pure Black African ancestors of the impure (<100% White) niece and nephew of the Prince of Wales, thrive in Great Britain. Which part of our shithole AFRICA is great?

"How Europe underdeveloped Africa." Dr Walter Rodney (1942–1980).

"Jews are very good with money." President Trump (45th).

Whose cash?

Bianca and Jared Kushner are Jews.

Bernard Madoff (1938–2021), Ghislaine Maxwell's dad, Ján Ludvík Hyman Binyamin Hoch (1923 -1991), and Judas Iscariot were Jews.

GIGANTIC yields of stolen lives of children of poor Africans, not feudal agriculture, lured the Jewish ancestors of Benjamin Disraeli (1804–1881) to Great Britain.

OYINBO OMO OLE: THIEVES—HABAKKUK.

https://medium.com/@mluther88983/vindictive-fury-of-a-satanic-wh...

## VINDICTIVE FURY OF A SATANIC WHITE FREEMASONS' NETWORK: RACIST MASON JUDGES

WEBNov 23, 2023 · WebSir Winston Churchill Based on accessible information, it is the absolute truth that District Judge Ayers of Bedford County Court in Bedfordshire, England, ...

BEDFORD, ENGLAND: District Judge Paul Robert Ayers, >70, a Mason, and the Senior Vice President of the Association of Her Majesty's District Judges, 3, St Paul's Square, MK40 1SQ, you will be free only when Nigerian, from shit hole Africa, dies, before then, the indiscreetly White Supremacist Satanic Legal System, overseen by FREEMASONS, which you served, will be uncovered, and irreversibly destroyed.

NHS/GDC: Freemason, Brother Richard William Hill, Senior NHS Postgraduate Tutor, Bedfordshire, fabricated reports and unrelentingly lied under oath—Habakkuk 1:4. A very, very, very, dishonest pure White Freemason. A crooked closeted hereditary racist FREEMASON.

IGNORANT DESCENDANTS OF THIEVES AND OWNERS OF STOLEN CHILDREN OF POOR PEOPLE - HABAKKUK.

BEDFORD, ENGLAND: District Judge Paul Robert Ayers, >70, a Mason, and the Senior Vice President of the Association of Her Majesty's District Judges, 3, St Paul's

Square, MK40 1SQ, apart from debt-collection, what was in NORWICH for functional semi-illiterate FREEMASON Solicitors to do? The universally acknowledged irrefutably superior skin colour that the very, very, very, fortunate wearer neither made nor chose, a huge stolen trust fund, and what else?

Before Slavery, what?

Then, there was only subsistence feudal agriculture.

"Agriculture not only gives riches to a nation, but the only one she can call her own." Dr Samuel Johnson

**TWENTY-SEVEN:** Kamala Harris did not say that Trump's administration packed courts with MEDIOCRE PURE WHITE JUDGES. "The best opportunity of developing academically and emotional." Bedford's District Judge Paul Robert Ayers, >70, a Mason, and the Senior Vice President of the Association of Her Majesty's District Judges, 3, St Paul's Square, MK40 1SQ. A brainless, unashamedly functional semi-illiterate, and opportunist RACIST pure White bastard.

An ultra-righteous descendant of very, very, very, nasty, merciless, and vicious racist murderers, nastier than Yevgeny Prigozhin (1961–2023), industrial-scale professional THIEVES, armed robbers. armed land grabbers, gun runners, opium merchants (drug dealers), and owners of stolen children of poor people, including the pure Black African ancestors of our impure Black Duchess, Meghan Markle (43% Nigerian), and her impure children (<100% White). Unlike Putin's Russia, there are no oil wells or gas fields in LUTON and where his own pure White father and mother were born, he is a functional semi-illiterate, he is relatively rich, and he dishonestly implied that he did not know that the pure White ancestors of his pure White mother and father were extremely nasty RACIST MURDERS, thieves, and owners of stolen children of poor people, including the pure Black African ancestors of the impure (<100% White) great grandchildren of Prince Phillip (1921–2021), the Duke of Edinburgh of Blessed Memory. Philippians 1:21: Phillip was a 33rd Degree Freemason (Scottish Rite).

Bedford's District Judge Ayers: White Skin and Stolen Trust …Amazon UK. https://www.amazon.co.uk › Bedfords-District-Judge-Ay…Buy Bedford's District Judge Ayers: White Skin and Stolen Trust Fund. Before Slavery, What?: 100% Genetic Nigerian Whistleblowing Mole by Ekweremadu, …£8.19.

ACCURATE SEERS: They foresaw that a pure White Welsh imbecile would be our England's Class Postgraduate Tutor, Oxford, so they embarked on armed robbery and dispossession raids in our own AFRICA, and whenever very, very, very, greedy racist pure White bastards, and those they armed, used guns to mercilessly slaughter our own African ancestors, they dispossessed them, and wherever armed racist pure White bandits and sea wolves robbed our own African ancestors, they took possession. Then, they were greedier than the grave and like death the insatiably greedy racist pure White bastards were never satisfied—Habakkuk 2:5, and they used yields of several continuous centuries of MERCILESS RACIST EVIL (stealing and slavery) to create a very, very, very, lavish Socialist Eldorado for millions of imbeciles, and they decommissioned natural selection, and they reversed evolution, and they made it possible for millions of imbeciles to breed more millions of imbeciles.

"An urgent need for depopulation." John Kerry.

John, castrate or sterile all imbeciles in Great Britain, including all crooked, functional semi-illiterate, and hereditary White Supremacist Freemason Judges.

Bedford's District JudgemPaul Robert Ayers, >70, a Mason, and the Senior Vice President of the Association of HHer Majesty's District Judges, 3, St Paul's Square, MK40 1SQ, our own money, NIGERIA (oil/gas), is by far more relevant to the economic survival of all your own White children than Freemasons' Kempston.

"The best opportunity of developing academically and emotional." Bedford's District Judge Paul Robert Ayers, >70, a Mason, and the Senior Vice President of the Association of HHer Majesty's District Judges, 3, St Paul's Square, MK40 1SQ.

## OUR ULTRA-RIGHTEOUS SENIOR DISTRICT JUDGE, ALBEIT ENGLAND'S CLASS.

An ignorant, ultra-righteous, and unashamedly functional semi-illiterate descendant of ultra-righteous THIEVES and owners of stolen children of poor people.

"Those who know the leasst obey the best." George Farquhar (1677–1707).

Perception is grander than reality.

His spinal cord is his highest centre.

His pure White skin concealed his impure dark black brain.

A very, very, very, hardened racist genetic alien with arbitrarily acquired camouflage English names; he gave the game away when he approved and immortalised what his functional semi-illiterate pure White mother and father spoke (deductible), which his poly-educated pure White superiors and supervisors in LUTON authorised.

HHJ Perusko studied law at Poly: Not Russell Group Second Class Alternative Education—Proverbs 17:16.

They love superiority, their brainless and baseless birth right, but they hate Freedom of Expression because they do not want their mentally gentler children and the imbeciles, they shepherd to know the truth.

Our own Nigerian Babies with huge oil wells and gas fields near their huts eat only 1.5/day in our own NIGERIA, two, too many, hereditary racist functional semi-illiterate pure White bastards whose pure White father and mother have never seen crude oil, and whose pure White ancestors, including the pure White Jewish ancestors of Benjamin Disraeli (1804–1881), were fed like battery hens with yields of stolen children of poor people, including the pure Black African ancestors of our impure Black Duchess, Meghan Markle (43% Nigerian), and her impure children (<100% White), thrive in our own Great Britain. Which part of our own shithole Africa is great?

Facebook

https://www.facebook.com/Daringtruths01/posts/oyinbo-ole-a-racis...

Daringtruths - Oyinbo ole: A racist white man. An ignorant.

WEBMay 13, 2023 · 3 Apr 2021 - District Judge Paul Ayers of Bedford County Court, the Senior Vice President of the Association of Her Majesty's District Judges. GDC:

Helen Falcon (MBE) lied on record. OUR DISHONEST RACIST. OUR WHITE WOMAN. BEDFORD, ENGLAND: Our semi-illiterate Freemason District Judge of our Empire of STOLEN AFFLUENCE. Our …

TWO: Matthew 5:9: "I just want the killings to stop." President Trump (45th). The probability that President Trump will make Jannah, with or without seventy-seven maidens, all very, very, very, libidinous virgins, should be higher than that of President Biden (46th), President Zelensky, and President Putin.


GDC: 37, Wimpole Street, London W1G 8DQ; 1, Colmore Square Birmingham, B4 6AA: Protecting Patients. Regulating the Dental Team. "This and no other is the root from which a tyrant springs, when he first appears he is a protector." Plato. Jonathan Martin, GDC Manager (caseworker), and alleged Rotarian (Freemasonry without voodoo and/or occultists' rituals) unrelentingly lied under oath. Poly-educated plebeian jobber parked his liability at the till of dentists' money. An ignorant ultra-righteous descendant of THIEVES and owners of stolen children of poor people, including the pure Black African ancestors of our impure Black Duchess, Meghan Markle (43% Nigerian), and her impure children (<100% White). OXFORD, ENGLAND: NHS/GDC. Mrs Helen Falcon, MBE, the archetypal Member of GDC Committee (former), vulgarly charitable Rotarian (Freemasonry without voodoo or occultists' rituals), a mere dmf (Community Dentist), the archetypal Postgraduate Dean, Oxford, and the spouse of Mr Falcon, unrelentingly lied under oath and/or on record—Habakkuk 1:4. A very, very, very, DISHONEST pure White cougar. A crooked closeted hereditary RACIST Member of the Most Excellent Order of our Empire of Stolen Affluence—Habakkuk. Jonathan Martin, GDC Manager (caseworker), and alleged Rotarian (Freemasonry without voodoo and/or occultists' rituals), poly-educated opportunist RACIST, let me tell you, reasoning and vision do not have finite boundaries, and the supernatural exists, and it is consistently accessible to those who stand where it can come—John 14:26. The fellow is who He says He is—John 14:6. "Jesus is the bedrock of my faith." HM (1926–2022). The mind that the NIGERIAN, from shithole Africa, did not choose is finer than the system you serve, and he has the power to use cogent facts and irrefutable evidence to irreversibly destroy you and it. OXFORD, ENGLAND: GDC/NHS/BDA/MPS, British Soldier, Territorial Defence, Stephanie Twidale (TD), unrelentingly lied under oath—Habakkuk 1:4. A very, very, very, dishonest pure White cougar. A crooked closeted hereditary racist British Soldier (Territorial Defence). The YANKEES are NATO, and absolutely everything else is an auxiliary bluff.

https://medium.com/@col.../dobern-property-limited-robert-ki...

DOBERN PROPERTY LIMITED: ROBERT KINGSTON, SOLICITOR

WEBAug 22, 2022 · District Judge Ayers, Bedford. Freemasons teach members secret handshakes, not grammar. GDC: Richard Hill fabricated reports and unrelentingly lied under oath. GDC: Kevin Atkinson (NHS …

BEDFORD, ENGLAND: District Judge Paul Robert Ayers, >70, a Mason, and the Senior Vice President of the Association of Her Majesty's District Judges, 3, St Paul's Square, MK40 1SQ, based on several decades of very, very, very, proximate observations and direct experiences, like FREEMASONS, vulgarly charitable ROTARIANS (Freemasonry without voodoo and/or occultists' rituals) are like RATS, and like RATS, they love to act without being seen, and like RATS, they are excessively stupid, so they defecate everywhere leaving tell-tale signs.

Based on several decades of very, very, very, proximate observations and direct experiences, they are THIEVES, and descendants of THIEVES, and the administration of their law is rooted in institutionalised RACIAL HATRED and FRAUD, and some hereditary White Supremacist Freemason Judges are in the loop of MERCILESS RACIST EVIL—Habakkuk.

"The white man is the devil." Elijah Mohammed (1897–1975).

Based on several decades of very, very, very, proximate observations and direct experiences, a White woman is not only a DEVIL (Jezebel), but she is also a THIEF, and she is thoroughly crazy.

OXFORD, ENGLAND: GDC/NHS/MPS/BDA, British Soldier, Stephanie Twidale (Territorial Defence), unrelentingly lied under oath—Habakkuk 1:4.

A very, very, very, DISHONEST pure White crooked cougar. A closeted hereditary racist British Soldier (Territorial Defence).

Based on very, very, very, proximate contact, the pure White woman stank; Stephanie Twidale (TD) had a distinct body odour.

"Britons stank." W.S.

Wole Soyinka, not William Shakespeare (1564–1616).

"We cannot fight for our rights and our history as well as the future until we are armed with weapons of criticism and dedicated consciousness." Edward Said.

EXISTENTIAL THREATS: Based on several decades of very, very, very, proximate observations and direct experiences, the survival of members of the baselessly and brainlessly self-awarded SUPERIOR RACE depend on the continuing persecution of AFRICANS, and the exploitation of AFRICA by very, very, very, greedy RACIST BASTARDS. Like their direct ancestors, they are greedier than the grave, and like death, the hereditary White Supremacist bastards will never be satisfied—
Habakkuk 2:5.

"How Europe underdeveloped Africa." Dr Walter Rodney (1942–1980).

**TWENTY-EIGHT:** BEDFORD, ENGLAND: District Judge Paul Robert Ayers, >70, a Mason, and the Senior Vice President of the Association of Her Majesty's District Judges, 3, St Paul's Square, MK40 1SQ, the legal system you served is absolutely irreparably BASTARDISED, indiscreetly dishonest, unashamedly mediocre, vindictive, potently weaponised, and institutionally RACIST — Habakkuk

BEDFORD, ENGLAND: District Judge Paul Robert Ayers, >70, a Mason, and the Senior Vice President of the Association of Her Majesty's District Judges, 3, St Paul's Square, MK40 1SQ, it is plainly deductible that you are worthy only because you are WHITE and ENGLAND is very , very, very, rich, apart from those, you are NOTHING. Perception is grander than reality. You are a LEECH, and the pure White ancestors of your own pure White father and mother were PURE WHITE THIEVES and owners of stolen children of very poor AFRICANS, including the pure Black African ancestors of Kamala Harris.

Then, ignorant hereditary RACIST pure White bastards (predominantly but not exclusively pure White) saw molecules, and they destroyed all NIGERIANS, from shithole Africa, who saw quarks.

NORTHAMPTON, ENGLAND: Senior NHS Nurse, Ms Rachael Bishop, unrelentingly lied under oath — Habakkuk 1:4. A very, very, very, dishonest pure White woman. A crooked closeted hereditary racist Senior NHS Nurse.

"A complaints such as Mrs Bishop's could trigger an enquiry." Stephen Henderson, LLM, BDS, Head at MDDUS, 1 Pemberton Row, London EC4A 3BG.

An unashamedly functional semi-illiterate, verifiably crooked, and hereditary racist pure White bastard.

His type killed the Indian dentist, only 42, albeit hands-off (remotely), with the mens rea hidden in the belly of the actus reus.

Google: Dr Anand Kamath, Dentist.

The only evidence of Stephen Henderson, LLM, BDS, Head at MDDUS, 1 Pemberton Row, London EC4A 3BG, very, very, very, High IQ is the STOLEN AFFLUENCE (yields of several centuries of merciless RACIST EVIL), which his thoroughly wretched pure White ancestors crossed the English Channels to latch onto.

It is deductible that since 1984, the only examination that the opportunist RACIST PURE WHITE BASTARD, Stephen Henderson, LLM, BDS, Head at MDDUS, 1 Pemberton Row, London EC4A 3BG, did not FAIL is the one he did not.

NIGER'S URANIUM: Russian and American (USA) troops are camped side by side at Niger's airport.

Then, very, very, very, greedy bastards carried and sold stolen children, now THIEVES steal our own AFRICA'S natural resources.

It is not the truth that substitution is true emancipation.

They accept to relinquish unfair advantageous positions only when they find alternative unfair advantageous positions.

"Moderation is a virtue only among those who are thought to have found alternatives." Henry Kissinger (1923–2023).

OUR OWN NIGERIA: SHELL'S DOCILE CASH COW SINCE 1956.

Unlike Putin's Russia, there are no oil wells or gas fields in Cavendish Square, Holborn, and where the pure White mother and father of Stephen Henderson, LLM, BDS, and Head at MDDUS, 1 Pemberton Row, London EC4A 3BG, were born.

Our own MONEY, our own NIGERIA (oil/gas), is by far more relevant to the economic survival of all the White children of Stephen Henderson, LLM, BDS, and Head at MDDUS, 1 Pemberton Row, London EC4A 3BG—than Nick Griffin's Llanerfyl Powys.

Facts are sacred.

Our imbecile, unashamedly functional semi-illiterate, and hereditary RACIST Freemason Senior District Judge of our Empire of Stolen Affluence—Habakkuk.

A brainless racist pure White bastard was granted the platform to display hereditary prejudice: The only evidence of his very, very, very, High IQ is the stolen affluence that his thoroughly wretched pure White ancestors crossed the English Channel, not that long ago, without luggage or decent shoes, to latch onto; they followed the money, stolen money, and our own money—yields of several continuous centuries of merciless RACIST EVIL.

1976–2022: Apart from his 5th Rate Poly Law Degree, almost everything else was the gift of Freemasonry's patronage.

Facts are sacred, and they cannot be overstated.

"Find the truth and tell it." Harold Pinter (1930–2008).

Medium

https://medium.com/@cole69915/poly-educated-racist-rubbish-226...

Poly-educated racist rubbish.—Medium

WEBMar 15, 2023 · It is plainly deductible that the white father and mother of Bedford's District Judge Paul Robert Ayers, > 70, a Mason, and the Senior Vice President of the Association of Her Majesty's …

'It was in 1066 that William the Conqueror occupied Britain, stole our land and gained control by granting it to his Norman friends, thus creating a feudal system we have not yet fully escaped.' Tony Benn (1925 -2014).

William the Conqueror stole from others what others had stolen from others.

**TWENTY-NINE:** Andrew Hurst (now, a senior Judge, albeit England's Class), probably restricted by poor self-education, threw flares, talked nonsense in an elementary attempt to conceal facts, and the pure White man lied when he stated that Mr Bamgbelu stated that Dr Richard Hill did not visit his practice in 2003.

Google: The White Judge Lied.

'Mr Bamgbelu has insisted that there was no practice visit in 2003 by Mr Hill.' Andrew Hurst (now, a senior Judge, albeit England's Class).

Andrew Hurst (now, a senior Judge, albeit England's Class) unrelentingly lied under oath.

Had he not been white British, and probably FREEMASON, he mightn't have gotten away with blatant dishonesty under oath.

Those regularly spun pure White privileged dullards (predominantly but not exclusively pure White) are amongst the dullest adult population in the industrialised world.

Ignorant ultra-righteous descendant of THIEVES and owners of stolen children poor people, including the poor Black African ancestors of our impure Black Duchess, Meghan Markle (43% Nigerian), and her impure children (<100% White).

Gigantic yields of centuries of merciless, racist evil immeasurably improved the standard of living of agricultural labourers from mainland Europe; it reversed their intellects: The sudden huge affluence weakened the common genetic pool.

GDC CHAMBERS, 20.11.2010:

CHAIRMAN (DR SHIV PABARY, MBE, JP): To clarify what we are talking about, you say no visit took place on that day, but there are bits of that form that you agree with?

BAMGBELU: Yes, I agree with.

CHAIRMAN (DR SHIV PABARY, MBE, JP): Are you saying that there was a visit, but later on, or there was no visit at all?

BAMGBELU: No, there was no visit at all on that day.

DAVID MORRIS (GDC's barrister): No visit on that day, but I think you told us that from time to time he would come and visit your surgery?

BAMGBELU: Yes, there was no visit on that day, but he would have come to my surgery. I can recall that when I moved, yes, he came to me, yes.

CHAIRMAN (DR SHIV PABARY, MBE, JP): Just to clarify, the actual issue of this report, is it the date that you dispute. The actual contents, what you just said about risk assessment, are true?

BAMGBELU: Yes.

*******

**THEY DO RACIAL HATRED AND FRAUD, AND THEY CALL IT LAW—HABAKKUK 1:4.**

Their law is equal for Blacks and Whites, but its administration is not, and the administration of the law is 'meat'.

"Rightful liberty is unobstructed action according to our will within limits drawn around us by the equal rights of others. I do not add 'within the limits of the law' because law is often but the tyrant's will, and always so when it violates the rights of the individual." President Thomas Jefferson (1743–1826).

Based on several decades of very, very, very, proximate observations and direct experiences, the administration of English Law is a very, very, very, potent weapon of a latent but raging RACE WAR.

They tell incompetent RACIST LIES in pursuant of the best interest of godforsaken imbeciles: Negrophobic Perjury guards Persecutory Negrophobia.

Skin colour that they neither made nor chose is universally acknowledged to be irrefutably SUPERIOR, but their intellects aren't, and they know.

For their LEGAL SYSTEM to work as designed, they must have SUPREME KNOWLEDGE (Matthew 2:16), and they don't, so they criminally steal yields of CHRIST-GRANTED talents of NIGERIANS, from shithole Africa.

OYINBO OLE: THIEVES—HABAKKUK.

BEDFORD, ENGLAND: NHS/GDC, Freemason, Brother, Richard William Hill fabricated reports and unrelentingly lied under oath—Habakkuk 1:4.

A very, very, very, dishonest pure White man. A crooked closeted hereditary RACIST Freemason. They hate us, and we know.

Facts are sacred, and they cannot be overstated.

Shiv Pabary, Member of the Most Excellent Order of our Empire of Stolen Affluence—Habakkuk, alleged Rotarian (Freemasonry without voodoo and/or occultists' rituals), our Justice of Peace (JP), and the archetypal Indian GDC Committee Chairman, unrelentingly lied under oath and/or record—Habakkuk 1:4. His Indian ancestors were incompetent RACIST LYING BASTARDS too, then, Indian Uncle Toms were accomplices of RACIST FRAUD in Colonial Africa—Habakkuk.

Google: The White Judge Lied.

Enduring residues of British Colonial Africa: Then, Indians were very, very, very, happy with any position underneath White Women, if White Men placed them above AFRICANS in the pecking order, and they find a very, very, very, dull, crooked, and mentally wonky Indian, and they adorn him with very, very, very, high titles, and he becomes Freemasons' Zombie Private Soldier.

'One witness at the Royal Commission in 1897 said that the ambition of Indians in Trinidad was 'to buy a cow, then a shop, and say: "We are no Nigg*rs to work in cane fields." Patrick French's 'Authorised Biography of V.S Naipaul: The World Is What It Is.'

In 2008, crooked and incompetently dishonest Richard Hill (FREEMASON) stated that he visited the surgery of the

Nigerian, from shithole Africa, on April 02, 2003, and produced a report. He did not state that he gave the alleged report to the NIGERIAN or anyone else. He lied, and lied, and lied again, under oath. Had he not been Pure White and Freemason, he would have been in trouble—
Habakkuk 1:4.

"Michael Jackson would have been found guilty if he'd been Black." Jo Brand.

Crooked and hereditary RACIST Richard Hill stated that he was asked to provide reports, in 2006. and the only evidence of NHS asking Richard Hill for reports was John Hooper's email of August 15, 2006, which was at the exclusive request of a British Soldier, Stephanie Twidale (our territorial defender). Three weeks later, on September 06, 2006, he released two separate reports he had spent three weeks fabricating, the reports of July 22, 2004, and the follow-up of an undisclosed date.

The criminally fabricated NHS reports of July 22, 2004, and the follow-up report of undisclosed date, which was requested by, and created for the crooked and closeted hereditary RACIST British Soldier (Territorial Defence), fitted seamlessly with what the crooked closeted hereditary racist bastard British Soldier, Stephanie Twidale (TD), the Hired NHS Liar was recruited to do.

Based on very, very, very, proximate observations and direct experiences, the creator hates them, so he blessed them with the universally acknowledged irrefutably superior skin colour, and He cursed the RACIST BASTARDS with an irreparably dark black brain.

The incompetently crooked and hereditary RACIST BASTARDS were two dull to discern the glaring flaws in their NEGROPHOBIC CONSTRUCTION.

If Pure White Freemason, Brother Richard Hill, Senior NHS Postgraduate Tutor, Bedfordshire, created very, very, very, adverse reports of inspections he allegedly carried out in July 2004, and the follow-up of undisclosed date, and he released these very, very, very, adverse cross-infection laden stereotypically dirty Nigg*r reports, more than two years later, on September 06, 2006, the half-wit Poly-educated wenches, libidinous Racist Cougar NHS Manager did not ask their hired incompetently DISHONEST racist bastard what he did about his very, very, very, adverse, and potentially life threatening findings—for almost three years (July 2004—February 2007)?

"The white man is the devil." Mohammed Ali (1942–2016).

**THIRTY:** Their type overwhelmed the Indian dentist, only 42, with unrelenting incompetent RACIST LIES, and

KILLED him, albeit hands-off (remotely), with the mens rea hidden in the belly of the actus reus. He will never return, so we must all go to him, including all the half-educated school dropouts, and White Supremacist bastards who, prematurely, sent the Indian who came to Great Britain for a better life—to infinite afterlife—2 Samuel 12:23. Poor fellow, he could not read his adversaries, so he did not realise their mind-set, so he did not realise that the RACIST BASTARDS would kill their own children for cash.

"He is a typical Englishman, usually violent and always dull." Wilde

Google: Mediocre GDC.

Google: Dr Anand Kamath, Dentist.

Based on cogent, irrefutable, and available evidence, Pure White Andrew Hurst (GDC's barrister, now a Senior Judge, albeit England's Class), lied implicitly under oath, when he stated that Mr Bamgbelu let it slip during cross examination that Dr Richard Hill visited his surgery in 2003.

If the Pure White mother of Pure White Andrew Hurst (GDC's barrister, now a Senior Judge, albeit England's Class), was properly married to his father on the day he was born, and he could prove that he did not unrelentingly lie under oath, he must sue the NIGERIAN, from shithole Africa.

'However, in the Panel questions Mr Bamgbelu let slip that the last time he had any involvement with Mr HILL was in

2003 (when being asked why not ask for assistance from the PCT as regards Clinical Governance in 2007).' Andrew Hurst, GDC chambers, 2009

Pure White Andrew Hurst (GDC's barrister, now a Senior Judge, albeit England's Class), unrelentingly lied under oath. Had he been black or Irish traveller or Gypsy, he mightn't have gotten away with INCOMPETENT RACIST LIES.

White Britons, Irish travellers and Gypsies are in the lowest third of those meeting academic targets at age 16—moron class or Gypsy class.

White British tribe is by far the most populous, but it is not the brightest.

The finest filtration of white Britons is not the brightest available in the UK; the brightest from any tribe or shade are the most desirable in the interest of the whole people.

Pure White Andrew Hurst (GDC's barrister, now a Senior Judge, albeit England's Class), is a white Briton, and together with Gypsies. and Pakistanis, he is a member of a group in the lowest third of those meeting academic targets at age 16; based upon very proximate observations and direct experiences, he seemed genetically disabled (mentally wonky).

Genetics: The Holy Grail.

Had Pure White Andrew Hurst (GDC's barrister, now a Senior Judge, albeit England's Class), had the intellect of a yellow man or woman, not the Albino Reggae man—I mean Chinese—he'd have realised that 'that day' referred to only one day (1/365).

Dr Stephen Hawking (1942–2018) implied that those who studied law related subjects in his school (not in his class) were so dull, they were not worthy of mention:

'In my school, the brightest boys did math and physics, the less bright did physics and chemistry, and the least bright did biology. I wanted to do math and physics, but my father made me do chemistry because he thought there would be no jobs for mathematicians.' Dr Stephen Hawking

Mr Bamgbelu stated that Dr Richard Hill visited his surgery in 2003.

In 2003, Mr Bamgbelu's surgery was on Bromham Road. Dr Richard Hill stated that he visited Mr Bamgbelu only once in 2003, at Bromham Road.

'I did not undertake any further inspections at Mr Bamgbelu's practice between 2003 and 2007.' Dr Richard Hill, withdrawal statement of 16.10.2008

The most important part of the 2003 visit and the alleged report of 02.04.2003 is that they were revealed to Mr Bamgbelu almost six years after the alleged findings.

Only those with Gypsy's brain (the last ethnic group on the list of those meeting academic targets at age 16), will allegedly find alleged concerns in 2003 and disclose the alleged concerns to the black man concerned six years after they were allegedly identified, and only after the GDC had charged the only black man in their midst with the alleged concerns; duration (almost six years) defeats the employment of the word, 'concern', and the fact is corroborated by the fact that Richard Hill stated that he did not visit the Negro for several years after the identification of the alleged concern.

Deluded, conceited, and ignorant privileged dullards, Jews and Romans, ordered His lynching because they did not understand what He said—Matthew 27:32–56.

They baselessly awarded themselves the monopoly of knowledge; the morons were oblivious to the notion of infinite vision and reasoning power.

The White British tribe, Gypsies and Pakistanis were in the same band, in the lowest third of the list of those hitting educational targets at age 16.

**THIRTY-ONE:** Cambridge University Educated Rich's Man Son, Sir, Mr. Justice Haddon-Cave, KC, which part of the Royal Courts of Justice, Strand, London WC2A 2LL, did the Pure White ancestors of your own Pure White father and mother buy, or which part of it preceded SLAVERY: Our Grand Cathedral Court or its chattels?

Pure White Man, let me tell you, the pure White ancestors of your own pure White father and mother were THIEVES, and owners of stolen children of people, including the pure Black African ancestors of our impure Black Duchess, Meghan Markle (43% Nigerian), and her impure children (<100% White).

Archie is impure (<100% White). Pure White Man, let me tell you, equitable, fair, and just reparation pends, and several centuries of unpaid interest accrue. You are very, very, very, rich ONLY because NIGERIAN (and others) descendants of the murdered and robbed do not, yet, have overwhelming leverage necessary to demand, and extract if need be, equitable, fair, and just REPARATION, and the full settlement of several centuries of unpaid interest.

********

GDC CHAMBERS 21.11.2008:

Pure White Andrew Hurst (GDC's barrister, now a Senior Judge, albeit England's Class): Until arguably April 2003, although we appreciate your answers that you do not accept you were visited in 2003.

BAMGBELU: Yes. It is important to yes, okay.

Pure White Andrew Hurst (GDC's barrister, now a Senior Judge, albeit England's Class): We will park that.

BAMGBELU: 2000/2001 is not part of it. In 2003, Mr Hill came to my practice when I moved from Grove Place. He wrote an inspection thing. He did not do it on that day, but even that visit that he did, there is nothing on it that is actually against me.

Pure White Andrew Hurst (GDC's barrister, now a Senior Judge, albeit England's Class): Quite. That is a point we will look at a bit later on. But taking it at its highest in the report in 2003, the only things he is particularly picking you up for is an absence of some of the documentation, is there not?

BAMGBELU: There were two things. I think he mentioned COSHH.

Pure White Andrew Hurst (GDC's barrister, now a Senior Judge, albeit England's Class): If you are agreeing with me, you do not necessarily need to go into a long explanation. Can we deal with it this way? We are agreeing that the April 2003 visit to Bromham Road, which you say did not happen but Council says it did whether it did or did not happen there is very little that Mr Hill picked up on. It was simply actually to do with documentation, the two things that you remembered.

BAMGBELU: That is right.

Pure White Andrew Hurst (GDC's barrister, now a Senior Judge, albeit England's Class): No problems in 2004 with Bedford?

BAMGBELU: Yes.

\*\*\*

"No problems in 2004 with Bedford?" Pure White Andrew Hurst (GDC's barrister, now a Senior Judge, albeit England's Class). A brainless racist pure White bastard: White skin, a huge stolen trust fund, and what else? Before Slavery, what? Of course, there was no problem in 2004. On August 15, 2006, at the request British Soldier, Stephanie Twidale (TD), John Hooper (NHS Manager) asked Richard Hill for reports, and about three weeks later, on September 06, 2006, Richard Hill released his incompetent NHS fabrications, the reports of the alleged visit of July 22, 2004 and the follow up report of undisclosed date, were withdrawn on October 16, 2008, more than years after the alleged visits, and more than two years after the incompetent RACIST FABRICATIONS were released by the NHS (Richard Hill), albeit only to White people, and almost immediately after the NIGERIAN, from shithole Africa, informed Alan Cohen (Dental Protection) that he was not in the UK of July 22, 2004, and his surgery was shut, and he had evidence.

Habakkuk: What do you own? You own NOTHING. Your principal assets are the universally acknowledged irrefutably superior skin colour that you neither made nor chose and the fact that England is very rich (the sixth largest economy in the world). You are a LEECH. Your ancestors were THIEVES and owners of stolen children of poor people, including the pure Black African ancestors of our impure Black Duchess, Meghan Markle (43%

Nigerian), and her impure children (<100% White). https://www.youtube.com/watch?v=BlpH4hG7m1A

They hate us, and we know. They love only MONEY, and we know that too. Then, they carried and sold millions of stolen children of poor people. Now they carry the natural resources of poor people. What they carry from our own AFRICA will change depending on their needs, but the carrying trade is immortal, as they need to carry scores of millions of imbeciles.

"They may not have been well written from a grammatical point of view but I am confident I had not forgotten any of the facts." Geraint Evans, England's Class Welsh Postgraduate Tutor, Oxford.

Nigerien children huge URANIUM MINES near their huts eat only 1.5/day in our own shithole Africa, a very, very, very, bellyful pure White Welsh imbecile who might not know the chemical formula for URANIUM, and whose pure White Welsh ancestors, including the pure White Welsh ancestors of Aneurin Bevan (1897–1960), were fed like battery hens with yields of stolen children of poor people, including the pure Black African ancestors of the impure (<100% White) niece and nephew of the Prince of Wales, was our Postgraduate Tutor, Oxford, Great Britain. Which part of our own shithole Africa is great?

Slavery preceded Aneurin Bevan's NHS, and paid for it.

Facts are sacred, and they cannot be overstated.

"The truth allows no choice." Dr Samuel Johnson

"The white man is the devil." Mohammed Ali (1942–2016)

Based on several decades of very, very, very, proximate observations and direct experiences, a White woman is not only a DEVIL (Jezebel), but she is also a THIEF, and she is thoroughly crazy.

OXFORD, ENGLAND: GDC/NHS/BDA/MPS, British Soldier, Stephanie Twidale (our territorial defender), unrelentingly lied under oath—Habakkuk 1:4.

A very, very, very, dishonest pure White cougar. A crooked closeted hereditary racist BRITISH SOLDIER (our territorial defender).

The YANKS are NATO, and absolutely everything else is an auxiliary bluff.

If FREEMASONS' occultists' rituals have progressive end products, and if they are as brave and as ethical as they seem to brag, they should, directly, use overwhelming extreme violence to evict Putin from Avdiivka, he used overwhelming extreme violence to convert it from bricks to rubble, and stole it.

"Ethical foreign policy." Robin Cook (1946–2005).

Based on several decades of very, very, very, proximate observations and direct experiences, their hairs stand on end when they are challenged by NIGERIANS; we and our type are the ones RACIST BASTARDS will beat up without the support of the YANKS.

<u>Medium</u>

https://medium.com/@mluther88983/racist-lies-of-crooked-kevin-at…

Racist Lies of Crooked Kevin Atkinson, Scottish Kev, Dentist

WEBNov 22, 2023 · Bedford. District Judge Ayers, 23/08/21. Justice, 23/08/21. Her Honour Judge Gargan, 23/08/21 . BEDFORD: District Judge, you're worthy because England is …

BEDFORD, ENGLAND: District Judge Paul Robert Ayers, >70, a Mason, and the Senior Vice President of the Association of Her Majesty's District Judges, 3, St Paul's Square, MK40 1SQ, White man, let me you, the most important part of the matter is money, and it is not the yield of talent, and the land on which your own pure White father and mother were born yields only FOOD. The pure White ancestors of your pure White father and mother were THIEVES and owners of stolen children of defenceless poor people. FREEMASONS: Vulgarly Charitable Antichrist White Supremacist bastards know how to deal with NIGERIANS who disagree with them, but they don't know how to repair the scatter-heads of their own pure White kindred—Habakkuk 1:4.

"They may not have been well written from a grammatical point of view but I am confident I had not forgotten any of the facts." Geraint Evans, England's Class Welsh Postgraduate Tutor, Oxford.

"The best opportunity of developing academically and emotional." Bedford's District Judge Paul Robert Ayers, >70, a Mason, and the Senior Vice President of the

Association of Her Majesty's District Judges, 3, St Paul's Square, MK40 1SQ.

Our imbecile Freemason Senior Judge of our Empire of Stolen Affluence.

A MORON MASON.

OYINBO OLE: No brain. Poor natural resources. Several continuous centuries of STEALING AND SLAVERY preceded the huge stolen fund. Before Slavery, what?

1976 – 2022: Having FAILED in practice, loads did, the functional semi-illiterate pure White rubbish parked his liability at the public till. A brainless racist pure White bastard. Unlike Putin's Russia, there are no oil wells or gas fields in Freemasons' Kempston and where his own pure White mother and father were born, he is a functional semi-illiterate, and he rich (relatively), and dishonestly implied that he did not know that the pure White ancestors of his own pure White mother and father were THIEVES and owners of stolen children of poor people, including the pure Black African ancestors of the impure (<100% White) niece and nephew of the Prince of Wales.

Google: White skin and stolen trust fund. Before Slavery, what?

The NHS reports of July 22, 2004, and the follow up of disclosed date, which were withdrawn by the NHS, in a signed statement of October 16, 2008, almost immediately after the Nigerian, from shithole Africa, informed Alan Cohen (Dental Protection) that he was not in the UK on

July 22, 2004, and his surgery was shut, and he had evidence.

'However, in the Panel questions Mr Bamgbelu let slip that the last time he had any involvement with Mr HILL was in 2003 (when being asked why not ask for assistance from the PCT as regards Clinical Governance in 2007).' Andrew Hurst, GDC chambers, 2009 The dialogue supra preceded the panel questions.

If, prior to the panel questions, Mr Bamgbelu admitted that Dr Richard Hill visited him in 2003, at Bromham Road, why does he need to let things slip during panel questions?

Pure rot!

A Moron Mason!

'Nothing that you will learn in the course of your studies will be of the slightest possible use to you in after life — save only this — if you work hard and diligently you should be able to detect when a man is talking rot, and that, in my view, is the main, if not the sole, purpose of education.' J. A. Smith (1869 – 1939), Oxford University Professor of Moral Philosophy

Bright is not white: Pure White skin seemed to conceal an impure dark black brain.

Andrew Hurst, white British barrister's memory was inferior, only his skin colour was good.

Their idea of a black man is he whose genes have endured several centuries of merciless, racist evil and concomitant reverse natural selection, often Blacks of Caribbean descent.

The Pure White Privileged Dullard (Andrew Hurst) seemed oblivious to the infinite reasoning power and vision of the supreme power that Hawking alluded to. He was a racist thug, and he lied, unrelentingly, implicitly under oath. If he could prove that he was not a closet racist thug, he must prove that he was not a liar, as not all liars are racists, but all racists are malicious liars.

**ABOUT THE AUTHOR:** The author attended Anglican Church Grammar School and the University of Lagos.